Disney's
TREASURE
PLANET
The Junior Novelization

PUFFIN BOOKS

Published by the Penguin Group
Penguin Books Ltd, 80 Strand, London WC2R 0RL, England
Penguin Putnam Inc., 375 Hudson Street, New York, New York 10014, USA
Penguin Books Australia Ltd, 250 Camberwell Road, Camberwell, Victoria 3124, Australia
Penguin Books Canada Ltd, 10 Alcorn Avenue, Toronto, Ontario, Canada M4V 3B2
Penguin Books India (P) Ltd, 11 Community Centre, Panchsheel Park,
New Delhi – 110 017, India
Penguin Books (NZ) Ltd, Cnr Rosedale and Airborne Roads, Albany, Auckland,
New Zealand
Penguin Books (South Africa) (Pty) Ltd, 24 Sturdee Avenue, Rosebank 2196, South Africa

Penguin Books Ltd, Registered Offices: 80 Strand, London WC2R 0RL, England

www.penguin.com

First published in the USA by Random House Children's Books, a division of Random
House, Inc., New York, and simultaneously in Canada by Random House of Canada
Limited, Toronto, in conjunction with Disney Enterprises, Inc. 2002
Published in Great Britain 2003
1

Set in 13 pt Times Ten

Made and printed in England by Clays Ltd, St Ives plc

British Library Cataloguing in Publication Data
A CIP catalogue record for this book is available from the British Library

ISBN 0–141–31622–5

Disney's
TREASURE
PLANET
The Junior Novelization

Adapted by Kiki Thorpe

Designed by Disney's Global Design Group

PUFFIN BOOKS

Prologue

There are nights when the etherium is as calm and peaceful as a pond on the Planet Pelsinor. Nights when the big merchant ships with their cargoes of Arcturian solar crystals can expect a smooth ride. But there was a time when even the calmest night could give way to the unexpected. Pirates, the enemies of all honest spacers, cruised the etherium's astral waves in search of merchant ships to plunder. And the most feared of all these pirates was the notorious Captain Nathaniel Flint.

Flint and his band of renegades would mysteriously swoop out of nowhere and overtake an unsuspecting merchant ship. Their cannonballs could rip through a ship's solar sails and shatter her masts. Once a ship was rendered helpless, the pirates stormed her decks in search of gold and gems. Then, gathering their spoils, they disappeared without a trace.

Flint's reign of terror lasted for nearly a hundred years. No merchant ship was safe. And then one day Flint and his crew simply disappeared, as if they'd dissolved into thin air.

For hundreds of years, stories of Flint's secret trove passed from spacer to spacer. The treasure was hidden somewhere at the furthest reaches of the galaxy, they said. Riches beyond imagination, the loot of a thousand worlds . . .

Chapter 1

Just outside the port town of Benbow on the planet Montressor, a fifteen-year-old boy named Jim Hawkins gripped the crossbar of a makeshift solar surfer. With energy panels for sails and a short, flat scrap of metal for the body, the craft hardly looked fit enough to cross the street. Still, Jim manned the solar surfer like an expert. He launched from the top of a cliff, then retracted the sail and tumbled through the air in a breathtaking free fall, executing a series of barrel rolls, back flips and twirls on his way down. Then, at the last second, Jim let out the sail. A gust of air caught him just a few feet above the ground. Jim straightened out and gunned the engine, sending the surfer flying through currents of air.

'*Whoo-hoo!*' Jim yelled. He smiled as the wind ruffled his brown hair. There was nothing he loved more than soaring through the etherium. Jim had spent his whole life listening to fantastic tales about spacers who travelled the galaxy in search of adventure. But for now, he was stuck on the sleepy old mining planet of Montressor. So Jim found his adventures where he could.

Up ahead, Jim saw the ruins of an old mine. A yellow-and-black-striped barricade blocked the entrance, warning that the area was off limits. Smashing through the barricade, Jim darted in and out among the rusting machinery. He skimmed his surfer along the edge of an old metal pipe, and sparks rained down behind him.

Just then, Jim spied the revolving wheels of a giant rock crusher. Amazingly, they were still moving. Small windows of light appeared briefly between the huge spokes of the heavy wheels as they passed each other. Jim's jaw set with determination as he aimed his surfer towards the small opening that would remain for only a moment. If he was too slow, he'd be crushed between the giant wheels. He charged forward at full throttle and darted through the narrow opening just before it closed. Jim let out a whoop as the heavy wheels churned on behind him.

But his victory was cut short by the sudden

wail of a police siren.

'Oh, great,' Jim groaned. He glided his solar surfer to a halt and watched grimly as two robot constables stepped from their vehicle to arrest him. This wasn't the first time he'd been caught by the police, and Jim knew what it meant. He would have to appear before the toughest judge in the galaxy: his mother.

Sarah Hawkins bustled around the dining room of the Benbow Inn, serving breakfast to her guests. The inn was full, and Sarah wished she had an extra hand to help with the work. She swiped a strand of brown hair away from her tired but pretty face and wondered where her son, Jim, was.

'I know... refill on the purp juice,' Sarah called to one of her customers. 'Coming right up, Mrs Dunwoody.' She lifted a large tray laden with food and carried it to a nearby table. A frog-like family looked up eagerly as Sarah served their breakfast.

'There we go, that's four powdered spheroids, two lunar eclipses . . .' Sarah placed a plate of iridescent pastries on the table and set two gelatinous blue fried eggs next to it. 'And a big bowl of Kirellian jellyworms for the big boy,' she

3

added, setting a bowl of squirming worms in front of the smallest alien.

The boy's green face lit up. 'Awesome!' he said, licking his lips and plunging his face into the bowl.

'Enjoy!' Sarah said as she moved on to the next table, where Dr Delbert Doppler sat. The dog-like alien was one of her best customers and a good friend. As she placed food and water bowls in front of him, Doppler carefully tucked his napkin into his collar.

'Sorry, Delbert, it's been a madhouse here all morning,' Sarah said apologetically.

'No problem, Sarah,' Doppler replied. He sniffed at his bowl of food and grinned. 'Ahhh,' he sighed. 'My Alponian chowder with the extra solaris seed. Yum!'

Just as Doppler brought a spoonful of chowder to his lips, he noticed a little alien child standing next to him.

'Hello, what brings you here, curious little one?' Doppler asked. The girl silently eyed Doppler's food. She was beginning to make him uncomfortable. 'Are your parents around?' he asked gently. The girl did not reply. 'What's the matter?' Doppler asked. 'Cat got your –'

At that moment, the little girl's long tongue

4

whipped out, snatching the food from Doppler's spoon. 'Yecch!' Doppler cried.

Sarah returned to his table just in time to see the little girl toddle away. 'Aw,' she said. 'They're so adorable at that age.'

Doppler frowned after the little girl. 'Yes,' he agreed, 'deplorable – er – adorable! Speaking of which, how's Jim doing?'

'Much better,' Sarah said as she collected an armload of dirty dishes from the table next to Doppler. 'I know he had some rough spots earlier this year, but I really think that he's starting to turn a corner...'

Just then, the door to the inn swung open. 'Mrs Hawkins,' said a robotic voice.

Sarah turned and saw Jim standing in the doorway, flanked by two robot constables. The dishes she was holding crashed to the floor.

'Jim!' she cried.

'Hmm ... wrong turn,' Doppler observed.

The robot constables rolled towards Sarah. 'We apprehended your son operating a solar vehicle in a restricted area,' one of the policemen informed Sarah.

Dismayed, Sarah looked at Jim. He shrugged and turned away.

'As you are aware, ma'am,' the first robot went on, 'this constitutes a violation of his probation.'

'Yes,' Sarah said. 'Yes, I understand, b-but could we just –'

'Pardon me, officers,' Doppler said, suddenly stepping forward. 'If I might interject here. I am the noted astrophysicist Dr Delbert Doppler. Perhaps you've heard of me?' The policemen stared at him blankly. 'No? Uh, I have a clipping.' Doppler began to fumble in his coat pocket.

'Are you the boy's father?' the first constable asked him sternly.

'Oh! Good heavens, no!' Doppler said with a shudder. 'Eew!'

'Oh, no, no – eew,' Sarah hurriedly agreed. 'He's just an old friend of the family.'

'Back off, sir!' the constable ordered Doppler.

'Thank you, Delbert,' Sarah told her friend. 'I will take it from here.'

'Well, Sarah, if you insist,' Doppler said as he hastily backed away from the robots. 'Don't ever let me do that again,' he whispered to Sarah.

'Due to repeated violations, we have impounded his vehicle. Any more slip-ups will result in a one-way ticket to juvenile hall,' the first constable said.

'Kiddie hoosegow,' the second added enthusiastically.

'The slammo,' the first officer declared. Jim glared at them, his cheeks burning.

'Thank you, officers,' Sarah said. She fixed Jim with a stern look. 'It *won't* happen again.'

'We see his type all the time, ma'am,' the first officer said.

'Wrong choices,' added the second officer.

'Dead-enders.'

'Losers.' With each word the robots uttered, Sarah's shoulders slumped a bit more.

'You take care now,' the first officer said cheerfully.

'Let's motor,' his partner said, and the two rolled out through the door. Sarah watched them leave, then turned back to the dining room. All the customers were staring at her and Jim. Embarrassed, Sarah pulled her son to the side of the room.

'Jim, I have had it!' she snapped. 'Do you *want* to go to juvenile hall? Is that it?'

The pleading note in her voice made Jim wince. He picked up a tray and began clearing a nearby table, trying to help.

'Jim, look at me!' Sarah cried. Jim said nothing,

but continued to pick up the dirty plates and glasses. Sarah heaved a sigh of exasperation. 'It's been hard enough keeping this place afloat by myself, without you –'

At last, Jim spun to face her. 'Mum, it was no big deal!' he cried. 'There was nobody around. Those cops just won't get off my . . .' Jim broke off. He could tell by his mother's expression that she didn't believe him. He turned away. 'Forget it.'

'Mithith Hawkinth!' Mrs Dunwoody lisped, waving her empty glass in the air. 'My juith!'

'Yes, I'll be right there, Mrs Dunwoody!' Sarah called to her. As she hurried towards the bar, she turned back to her son. 'Jim, I just don't want to see you throw away your entire future,' she said sadly.

Jim looked down at the dirty dishes in his hands and heaved a sigh. 'Yeah,' he muttered miserably, turning towards the kitchen. '*What* future?'

Chapter 2

Jim sat on the thatched roof of the Benbow, staring at the gathering storm clouds. Thunder rumbled in the distance, and a few droplets of rain splattered on to the roof next to him. Jim knew he should go inside, but he wasn't yet ready to face his mother again – he couldn't stand to see the disappointment in her eyes. Unfortunately, he seemed to be seeing it more and more often these days. He never meant to upset his mother, but even when he went out of his way to avoid trouble, it seemed to find him anyway.

The rain started to come down harder, and a flash of lightning lit the sky. Jim sighed and had begun to climb down from the roof when suddenly he heard a familiar voice coming from one of the windows. He peered inside. Doppler and Sarah were sitting together, talking.

'I really don't know how you manage it, Sarah,' Doppler said. 'Trying to run a business while raising a felon ... er ... *fellow* like Jim.'

'Manage it?' Sarah replied. 'I'm at the end of my rope. Ever since his father – well, Jim's just never recovered.'

Listening, Jim shifted uncomfortably. Jim and his mother never talked about his father, who'd left them to sail the galaxy when Jim was only nine. But Jim still thought about him nearly every day. He hadn't realized that his mother knew.

'And you know how smart he is,' Jim heard Sarah go on. 'He built his first solar surfer when he was *eight*! And yet he's failing at school, he's constantly in trouble, and when I talk to him, he's like a stranger to me.' She sighed, and Jim felt a pang of guilt. 'I don't know, Delbert. I've tried everything I could think of,' Sarah said. 'If something doesn't change soon ...'

Suddenly, the roar of an engine drowned out Sarah's voice. Jim turned and saw an out-of-control space cruiser careering towards the wooden docks near the Benbow Inn. With an ear-shattering crash, the cruiser slammed into one of the docks.

'Whoa!' Jim slid off the roof and hurried down

the hill to the ship. He peered into its smoking fuselage. 'Hey, mister!' Jim called. 'You OK in there?'

A clawed hand pressed against the glass and the cruiser's hatch flew open. Jim drew back in surprise as a grizzled, turtle-like alien dragged himself from the cabin and looked around in a daze. When his eyes lit on Jim, he grabbed the startled boy by the collar.

'He's a-comin'!' the alien moaned, his eyes rolling wildly. 'Can ya hear 'im? Those gears and gyros clickin' and whirrin' like the devil himself!'

'Hit your head pretty hard there, didn't ya?' Jim said nervously, trying to pull himself free from the strange alien.

'He's after me chest, that fiendish cyborg and his band o' cutthroats!' the alien croaked as he released Jim. Reaching into the cabin of his cruiser, the alien drew out a small trunk and hoisted it on to his shoulder. 'But they'll have to pry it from ol' Billy Bones's cold, dead fingers afore I –'

The alien broke off in a coughing fit, then staggered and collapsed in a heap. The chest thudded to the ground next to him.

Jim hesitated, staring down at Bones. Heavy

drops of perspiration studded the alien's brow. Jim pressed his lips together. He couldn't just leave the old coot there to die.

'C'mon, give me your arm,' Jim said as he lifted Bones to his feet. Supporting Bones with one arm and carrying the chest with the other, he staggered up the hill towards the Benbow Inn.

'Mum's gonna love this,' Jim muttered to himself.

Inside the inn, Sarah slumped in a chair and stared out of the window at the pouring rain.

'Thanks for listening, Delbert,' Sarah told her friend.

Doppler patted her shoulder. 'It's going to be OK. You'll see,' he said gently. As Doppler walked towards the door, Sarah picked up the hologram charm she wore on a chain round her neck and gazed sadly at the images of Jim as a small boy. She sighed, remembering the sound of his giggles when she used to read to him at night. How long had it been since she'd heard him laugh? She couldn't remember.

'I keep dreaming that one day I'll open that door and there he'll be, just the way he was,' Sarah said wistfully. 'A smiling, happy little boy holding a new pet and begging me to let him keep it.'

Suddenly, there was a thump at the door. Doppler opened it – and stumbled back in surprise. A flash of lightning revealed Jim, drenched to the bone, with a hulking body slung over his shoulder!

Sarah gasped. 'James Pleiades Hawkins,' she began. 'What have –'

'Mum, he's hurt – *bad*!' Jim interrupted.

Bones tumbled on to the floor, gasping and wheezing. 'Me chest, lad!' he cried. Jim hurriedly set down the chest. Bones typed in a secret code and the lock opened. The alien reached into the chest and pulled out a bundled object. His fingers shook as he held it out to Jim.

'He'll be comin' soon,' Bones rasped. 'I can't let him find this.'

'*Who's* coming?' Jim asked.

Bones grabbed Jim by the collar and yanked him so close that Jim could feel the old alien's breath on his face. 'The *cyborg*,' Bones whispered urgently. '*Beware the cyborg!*'

As the words left his lips, Bones's eyes closed and he slumped to the floor. Jim clutched the bundle and stared as the last sigh escaped Bones's body.

Suddenly, Jim heard a low rumbling sound more ominous than thunder. Sarah, Jim and Doppler looked at one another, their eyes wide. Jim raced to the window. Through the pouring rain, he could make out the dark shape of a schooner docked in the port below. A group of figures clambered down from its deck. Jim knew what they were – pirates!

Sarah hurried to Jim's side and gasped in horror. The pirates were climbing the hill towards the inn.

'Quick! We gotta go!' Jim grabbed his mother's hand and pulled her up the inn's stairway.

Doppler stood frozen, staring out of the window. Just then, a laser bolt shot through the window and blew a hole in the books Doppler held under his arm. 'I believe I'm with Jim on this one!' he cried, dropping the books and dashing up the stairs. A second later, the door burst open. Space pirates poured into the room.

'Where is it?' one of them growled.

The others moved swiftly, ransacking the inn. 'It's got to be here somewhere!' one roared, overturning chairs and tables.

'Find it!' another cried. They used their swords to slash through pillows and bags of food in search of Billy Bones's bundle.

Suddenly, another sound rose above the pirates' rough cries. The pirates' leader strode through the door of the inn, his limbs clicking and whirring. He stopped in the centre of the room, casting a long shadow over Bones's body.

Upstairs in the inn's attic, Doppler threw open a window and called down to his bullyadous, the large creature that pulled his carriage.

'Delilah! Stay . . . Don't move . . . ' he commanded.

Sarah, Jim and Doppler climbed to the ledge of the attic window. Their only escape was to jump down to Doppler's carriage three storeys below. But Sarah clung to the windowsill, terrified.

'Don't worry, Sarah,' Doppler said. 'I'm an *expert* in the laws of physical science!'

'No, no, no! Please, I can't!' she cried.

'On the count of three,' Doppler said, taking her hand. 'One . . . two . . .'

But Doppler never reached three, because just then, Jim saw the pirates' shadows moving up the stairs. They were almost to the attic! Thinking quickly, Jim leaped through the window, pushing his mother and Doppler out ahead of him. The three figures tumbled through the air and landed with a thud in Doppler's carriage.

'Go, Delilah! *Go!*' Doppler shouted. As the carriage tore down the road, Jim and Sarah looked back over their shoulders. The Benbow Inn was engulfed in flames. Jim cast a sideways glance at his mother, reading the look of horror written on her face. He knew what she was thinking – that everything she'd worked for was gone, transformed into smoke and ashes. Jim's chest felt tight, and he wished desperately that he'd never seen Billy Bones, never brought him to the Benbow.

Jim pulled Billy Bones's bundle from his coat pocket and unwrapped it. Hidden beneath the tattered cloth was a small gold sphere engraved with strange markings. Jim turned the object over in his hands. What was this mysterious orb?

And why were those pirates after it?

Chapter 3

Later that evening, Jim and Sarah sat before a crackling fire in Doppler's study. The rain had let up, and now a bright crescent moon shone through the window. Jim looked around the room at the scientist's impressive collections of books, star charts and astrolabes. But Sarah only stared miserably into the flames.

'I just spoke with the constabulary,' Doppler told her. 'Those blackguard pirates have fled without a trace,' he said. He went to Sarah and knelt at her side. 'I'm sorry, Sarah, I'm afraid the old Benbow Inn has burned to the ground.'

Sarah looked at Jim, her eyes filled with grief. What would she do now? They had no place to live and no money to rebuild the inn. Doppler brought her a cup of tea, and Jim wrapped a blanket round his mother's shoulders.

Jim picked up the gold sphere and peered at it. The pirates had destroyed his home for *this*? He began to fiddle with it, running his fingers over the strange markings.

'Well, certainly a lot of trouble over that odd little sphere,' Doppler said. 'Those markings baffle me. Unlike anything I've ever encountered. Even with my vast experience and superior intellect, it would take me years to unlock its – *hey!*'

Doppler jumped as a spark flew from the glowing sphere. He couldn't believe his eyes. Jim had unlocked the orb in mere seconds! As Jim and Doppler leaned closer, smart pixels flew from the orb, creating a three-dimensional image of planets and stars. The glowing image filled the room, rotating round their heads. Doppler dimmed the lights so they could see it better.

'Why, it appears to be some kind of map!' he exclaimed. He looked closely at a planet. 'Wait, wait, wait! This is *us*. The planet Montressor.' Doppler touched the planet – and the map came alive! In an instant, the pixels formed starfields, which zoomed around Doppler, Jim and Sarah.

'That's the Magellanic Cloud, and – *oh!*' Doppler squealed with excitement. 'The Coral Galaxy . . . the Cygnus Cross . . . and that's the

Calyan Abyss!' Suddenly, a luminescent green orb came into view. The scientist caught his breath. 'Wait . . . What's this? Why, it's . . .'

The orb projected an image of a glowing, green two-ringed planet. Jim's face lit up in awe. 'Treasure Planet!' he said. He was certain of it. Ever since he was a small boy, Jim had lived and breathed the legend of Treasure Planet. And there it was – the image of the planet was just as he'd always pictured it.

'Flint's trove? The loot of a thousand worlds!' Doppler cried. 'Do you know what this means?'

Jim grinned. 'It means that all that treasure's only a boat-ride away.'

The map swirled in front of Doppler's astonished face. 'Whoever brings it back would hold an eternal place atop the pantheon of explorers. He'd be able to experience –' Suddenly the room went dark as the last of the map spiralled back into the sphere. Doppler's smile disappeared. 'What just happened?' he asked.

Jim stared, wide-eyed, at the closed sphere in his hand. 'Mum, this is it!' he cried. 'This is the answer to all our problems!'

'Jim, there is absolutely no way –' Sarah began.

'Don't you remember?' Jim interrupted her.

'All those stories!'

'That's all they were!' Sarah told him. 'Stories!'

But Jim shook his head. He'd always known that Treasure Planet was real – and now he was holding the proof right in the palm of his hand! 'With that treasure we could rebuild the Benbow a hundred times over!' he cried.

'Well, this is . . . it's just . . .' Sarah stammered. She turned to Doppler. 'Delbert, would you please explain how ridiculous this is?'

Doppler nodded. 'It's totally preposterous, traversing the entire galaxy alone . . .'

'Now at last we hear some sense,' Sarah said.

'That's why *I'm* going with you,' Doppler finished. Jim gaped at him in surprise. Doppler had grabbed a suitcase and was dashing around the room, stuffing books and clothing inside.

'Delbert!' Sarah exclaimed.

'I'll use my savings to finance an expedition!' he told her. 'I'll commission a ship, hire a captain and a crew!'

Sarah stared at him. 'You're not serious,' she said.

Doppler turned to face her. His eyes were wild with excitement. 'All my life I've been waiting for an opportunity like this, and here it is, screaming,

'"Go, Delbert! Go, Delbert! Go –"'

'OK,' Sarah said, cutting him off. 'You're *both* grounded.'

'Mum, look,' Jim said suddenly. 'I know that I keep messing everything up. I know I've let you down, but this is my chance to make it up to you – to set things right.' Sarah's face softened. Doppler pulled her aside.

'You said yourself you've tried everything,' he told her gently. 'There are much worse remedies than a few character-building months in space.'

Sarah thought for a moment. 'Are you saying this because it's the right thing, or because *you* really want to go?' she asked finally.

'I really, really, really, *really* want to go,' Doppler answered. '*And* it's the right thing.'

Resigned, Sarah turned back to her son. 'Jim, I don't want to lose you,' she said quietly. She brushed his hair away from his eyes.

Jim looked his mother in the eye. 'Mum, you won't,' he said slowly. 'I'll make you proud.'

Chapter 4

Several days later, Jim and Doppler sat aboard a space ferry on their way to Crescentia, the giant spaceport from which they would depart on their journey. From a distance, the crescent-shaped port looked like a glowing sliver of moon. But as they approached, Jim could see that the port was actually a many-layered network of docks, all crowded with spaceships. As the space ferry touched down, Jim shivered with excitement. Looking around the massive spaceport, he felt that anything could happen. He hurried down the gangplank, eager to reach the docks and whatever adventure awaited him there.

At the bottom, Jim paused and looked around breathlessly. Aliens of every shape and colour, speaking hundreds of different languages, were scurrying this way and that, securing rigging, scraping hulls and bartering for goods. He stopped and watched, fascinated, as two spacers in heavy coats and stocking caps pulled star matter out of a net. Even the air smelled different here, Jim thought. It was fresh and brisk and had a mysterious tang, unlike anything he'd ever smelled on dreary old Montressor. Jim felt like shouting with joy.

'Jim!' Doppler's voice cut into his thoughts. Jim turned in time to see Doppler waddle down the gangplank, dressed in an outdated space suit and clanking with every step. He was so loaded down with gear that he could barely walk. 'Jim!' he called. 'Oh, Jim, wait for me!'

Jim grinned and shook his head as Doppler caught up to him.

'Well, this should be a wonderful opportunity for the two of us to get to know one another,' Doppler said. 'You know what they say: Familiarity breeds . . . uh, well . . . contempt. But in our case –'

'Look, let's just find the ship,' Jim interrupted. He hurried over to two alien longshoremen to ask directions.

'Second berth on your right,' one alien told him in a voice that was gruff but polite.

Doppler scurried awkwardly after Jim as they moved through the docks. 'It's the suit, isn't it?' he asked. 'I should never have listened to that pushy two-headed saleswoman. One head said it fitted, and the other said it was my colour. I get so flustered and – Oh!' Doppler's jaw dropped. Before them a huge, three-tiered solar galleon gleamed in the sunlight. It was the RLS *Legacy*, the ship Doppler had hired. It was the grandest ship either Jim or Doppler had ever seen, and it was already bustling with activity.

Together they hurried up the gangplank on to the ship. On deck, a tough-looking crew of alien spacers raced fore and aft, readying the ship for launch. Mr Arrow, a square-jawed, rock-skinned alien in an officer's uniform, stood in the middle of the deck, shouting commands.

'Stow those casks forward! Heave together now!'

'Good morning, Captain!' Doppler called to him. 'Everything shipshape?'

'Shipshape it is, sir,' Arrow replied. 'But I'm not the captain. The captain's aloft.' He pointed. Jim and Doppler looked up towards the rigging and saw a slim, cat-like creature also in an officer's uniform. She swung down the ropes and landed gracefully on the deck.

'Mr Arrow, I've checked this miserable ship from stem to stern and, as usual, it's spot on. Can you get nothing wrong?' she said to the alien.

'You flatter me, Captain,' Arrow replied.

'Dr Doppler, I presume,' the captain said, turning to Doppler and Jim.

'Why, yes . . . I . . . ' Doppler stammered in surprise. He hadn't realized a female would be running the ship. Much less a *feline* female.

The captain smiled and shook his hand.

'I'm Captain Amelia,' she said. 'Late of a few run-ins with the Procyan Armada. Nasty business, but I won't bore you with my scars. You've met my first officer, Mr Arrow.' She gestured to the stony alien at her side. 'Sterling, tough, dependable, honest, brave and true.'

'Please, Captain,' Arrow said modestly.

'Oh, shut up,' Captain Amelia told him. 'You know I don't mean a word of it.'

As they talked, Jim gazed around the ship. Its polished, caramel-coloured wooden decks ran hundreds of feet from stem to stern. Elaborate webs of rigging hung from the masts and, high above, the ship's bright flag snapped loudly in the wind. Jim sighed with satisfaction. It was just the sort of ship he'd always dreamed of sailing. For a moment, he imagined himself at the helm, steering the giant vessel through the etherium. But suddenly, his thoughts were interrupted.

'May I introduce you to Jim Hawkins,' Doppler was saying to Captain Amelia. 'Jim, you see, is the boy who found the treasure m–' Before he could finish, Amelia clapped a paw over his mouth.

'Doctor, *please*!' she said. She looked over her shoulder to make sure no one was listening, then said in a low voice, 'I'd like a word with you in my stateroom.'

Doppler, Arrow and Jim followed the captain to her quarters. She shut the door behind them, then looked sternly at Doppler.

'Doctor, to mewl and blabber about a treasure map in front of this particular crew demonstrates a level of ineptitude that borders on the imbecilic,' she said crisply, then added, 'And I mean that in a very caring way.'

'Imbecilic, did you say?' the doctor spluttered in response, but Amelia ignored him.

'May I see the map, please?'

Jim glanced at Doppler, then reluctantly pulled the map from his pocket and tossed it to Captain

Amelia. 'Here.'

The captain unlocked her gun cupboard and placed the map inside. 'Fascinating,' she said drily. 'Mr Hawkins, in future you will address me as "Captain" or "ma'am". Is that clear?'

Jim scowled at her, but the captain's gaze didn't falter. 'Yes, ma'am,' he replied finally.

Amelia smiled and locked the doors of the cupboard. 'That'll do. Gentlemen, this must be kept under lock and key when not in use. And Doctor, again, with the greatest possible respect, zip your howling screamer.'

'Captain, I assure you –' Doppler began.

'Let me make this as monosyllabic as possible,' Amelia snapped, cutting him off. 'I don't much care for this crew you hired. They are . . .' She turned to her first mate. 'How did I describe them, Arrow? I said something rather good this morning before coffee.'

'A ludicrous parcel of drivelling galoots, ma'am,' Arrow answered promptly.

'There you go – poetry!' Amelia's sly green eyes twinkled.

Doppler's face turned red. 'Now see here!'

'Doctor, I'd love to chat – tea, cake, the whole shebang – but I have a ship to launch.' She glanced at Doppler's space suit and cocked an eyebrow. 'And you've got your outfit to buff up,' she added. 'Mr Arrow, please escort these two neophytes down to the galley straight away. Young Hawkins will be working for our cook, Mr Silver.' Amelia turned sharply and walked away.

'Wait!' Jim cried. 'What? The cook?'

But Amelia was already gone.

Chapter 5

Mr Arrow led the way down a narrow gangway to the ship's galley. Jim and Doppler followed, still smarting from their run-in with Captain Amelia.

'That woman . . . ' Doppler fumed, '. . . that *feline*! Who does she think is working for whom?'

Jim shook his head angrily. 'It's *my* map and she's got me clearing tables –'

'I'll not tolerate a cross word about our captain,' Arrow interrupted. 'There's no finer officer in this or any galaxy.'

As they entered the ship's cluttered kitchen, Jim could hear someone whistling. He peered through the steam rising from the pots, trying to make out the figure standing at the stove.

'Mr Silver?' Arrow called.

The whistling stopped and a tall man turned

towards them. Through the steam, Jim could see the silhouette of his broad-shouldered body.

'Why, Mr Arrow, sir!' Silver cried with mock alarm. 'Bringin' such fine-lookin', distinguished gents to grace my humble galley! Had I known, I'd have tucked in me shirt!'

The cook stepped out of the steam towards them and Jim caught his breath sharply. The entire right side of Silver's body was mechanical! In place of one arm, one leg and one eye, he had gears, ratchets and flywheels.

'A cyborg!' Jim muttered suspiciously to himself, remembering Billy Bones's warning.

'May I introduce Dr Doppler, the financier of our voyage,' Arrow said to Silver.

Silver ran his laser eye over Doppler's space suit. He whistled. 'Love the outfit, Doc!'

'Well, thank you,' Doppler replied. 'Uh . . . love the eye.' He gestured to Jim. 'This young lad is Jim Hawkins.'

'Jimbo,' Silver said, extending his right hand, from which a number of kitchen gadgets protruded. Jim looked at it warily. Silver quickly transformed the gadgets into a claw-like metal hand. Jim frowned at it and kept his arms at his sides.

'Now, don't be too put off by this hunk o' hardware!' Silver told Jim. In a flash, his hand turned into a large cleaver. Quick as a wink, Silver diced a pile of vegetables. 'Whoa!' Silver pretended to chop off his other hand, then popped the hand back out his sleeve. He winked at Jim.

'These gears have been tough gettin' used to, but they do come in mighty handy from time to time.' Silver cracked some eggs into a pan, then used his hardware hand to light a flame underneath it. He flicked his hand again and a ladle popped out. Silver scooped stew into two bowls and handed them to Jim and Doppler. 'Have a taste of me famous bonzabeast stew!'

Doppler sniffed the stew, then cautiously tasted it. His face broke into a smile. 'Delightfully tangy, yet robust,' he declared.

'Old family recipe,' Silver told him. Just then, an eyeball floated to the top of Doppler's bowl. 'In fact,' Silver added, 'that was part of the old family.' He plucked the eyeball from the soup and popped it into his mouth. Doppler looked at him in horror. 'Just kiddin', Doc,' said Silver. 'I'm nothin' if I ain't a kidder.' He winked at Jim. 'Go on, Jimbo! Have a swig!'

Jim looked down at his bowl, reluctant to taste

the stew. Suddenly, his spoon opened its mouth and took a big gulp! Jim quickly dropped the spoon, which transformed into a pink blob of protoplasmic jelly. The blob smiled at him.

'Morph, you jiggle-headed blob o' mischief! So that's where you was hiding!' Silver scolded.

Morph morphed into a straw and slurped up the rest of the soup in Jim's bowl.

'What *is* that thing?' Jim asked.

Morph floated over and perched on Jim's finger. Suddenly, he transformed into a miniature replica of Jim, mirroring the boy's stunned expression.

'He's a . . . morph! I rescued the little shape-shifter on Proteus One,' Silver explained cheerfully. 'He took a shine to me. We've been together ever since.' Jim and Doppler watched, amazed, as Morph floated back to Silver. Silver rubbed Morph's belly and the creature wriggled like a happy puppy.

Just then, the ship's whistle blew. 'We're about to get under way,' Arrow informed them. 'Would you like to observe the launch, Doctor?'

Doppler's face lit up. 'Would I? Does an active galactic nucleus have superluminal jets?' Everyone just stared at him. 'I'll follow you,' he told Arrow sheepishly.

Silver helped himself to a mouthful of stew as Doppler and Arrow headed back up to the deck. Jim started to follow, but Arrow stopped him. 'Mr Hawkins will stay here, in *your* charge, Mr Silver,' Arrow said.

Phhhhht! Silver spat out his stew in surprise. 'Beggin' your pardon, sir,' he spluttered, 'but –'

'Captain's orders!' Arrow told him. 'See to it the new cabin boy's kept busy.' He turned and headed up the gangway with Doppler on his heels.

Alone, Jim and Silver sized each other up. Then Silver shrugged. 'Well, who be a humble cyborg to argue with a cap'n?' He turned back to his cooking.

Although the cyborg seemed friendly, Jim was wary. He decided to test Silver to see what he knew about Billy Bones and the treasure map. Slyly, he reached into a nearby barrel and pulled out a round purple fruit.

'You know,' he said casually, 'these purps are kind of like the ones back home, on *Montressor*.' Jim gave the word a subtle emphasis as he eyed Silver and asked, 'You ever been there?'

'Can't say as I have, Jimbo,' Silver replied.

'Come to think of it, just before I left, I met this

old guy who was, uh, kinda looking for a cyborg buddy of his,' Jim added.

Silver peered into a steaming soup pot. 'Is that so?'

Had there been a slight waver in the cyborg's voice just then? Jim wasn't sure. He decided to forge ahead. 'Yeah. What was the old salamander's name?' Jim pretended to search his memory. 'Oh, yeah. *Bones*. Billy Bones.' He watched Silver carefully to see his reaction, but the cyborg didn't flinch.

'Bones?' Silver repeated. 'It ain't ringin' any bells. Musta been a different cyborg. There's a slew of cyborgs roamin' this port.'

On the deck above, the launch whistle blew again. 'Prepare to cast off!' Arrow shouted. Jim's face fell. Here he was, on his first great adventure, and he was stuck in the kitchen. He might as well have stayed on Montressor.

Silver smiled at him. 'Off with ya now and watch the launch,' he said. 'There'll be plenty o' work waitin' for ya afterwards.'

Jim hesitated. He was still suspicious of Silver, but he didn't want to miss the ship's launch. Finally, his eagerness got the better of him, and he turned and bolted up the gangway.

As soon as Jim was gone, Silver's smile faded. He fed a scrap to Morph and narrowed his eyes thoughtfully.

'We best be keepin' a sharp eye on this one, eh, Morph?' Silver said softly. 'We wouldn't want him strayin' into things he shouldn't.'

Chapter 6

In the crow's nest, Onus, the ship's lookout, held a spyglass to one of his many eyes. 'Vee are all clear, Capteen!' he called in a thick Zandarian accent.

Below him on the ship's bridge, Amelia turned to Arrow. 'Well, my friend, are we ready to raise this creaking tub?'

'My pleasure, Captain,' Arrow said. '*All hands to the stations!*' he called, and the crew hurried to obey. '*Smartly, now! Loose all solar sails!*'

The crew hauled the lines, and the huge solar sails unfurled along the masts like fans unfolding. As the sails caught the bright sunlight, their surfaces began to shimmer, holding and storing the light as power. Slowly, the ship rose and moved away from the dock.

'*Lay aft to the braces! Brace up!*' called Arrow.

The RLS *Legacy* cast away her tethers and glided up into the etherium.

Jim felt his spirits start to lift. He felt lighter than air, almost as though he were floating. When he looked down, he realized that he *was* floating! In fact, the entire crew was floating – once the ship had left the spaceport, they had left gravity as well.

'Mr Snuff, engage artificial gravity,' Amelia commanded the alien standing next to her. Snuff flipped a switch, sending everyone plummeting back to the deck. Doppler landed in a heap at the captain's feet.

Amelia turned to the multi-armed helmsman. 'South by south-west, Mr Turnbuckle. Heading, two-one-zero-zero.'

'Aye, Cap'n. Two-one-zero-zero,' Turnbuckle repeated. With one of his hands, he pulled a lever. An electromagnetic power field washed over the deck.

'Full speed, Mr Arrow, if you please,' the captain ordered.

'*Take her away!*' Arrow called.

Amelia turned to Doppler. 'Brace yourself, Doctor,' she said. Before Doppler could respond, the ship lurched forward at an incredible speed, sending him tumbling against the ship's rail.

Jim hung from the ratlines, watching with wide-eyed wonder as they hurtled through the cosmos. He spied a whale-like creature with mottled pink and blue skin flying through space beneath them.

'Whoa!' he cried as a whole school of the creatures soared past, fanning the air with their giant fins.

'Upon my word!' Doppler exclaimed from his place at the railing. 'An *orcus galacticus*!' He aimed his camera, calling out, 'Smile!'

'Doctor, I'd stand clear of that,' Amelia warned just as a space whale spouted from its blowhole, drenching Doppler in slimy nebula spray. Amelia chuckled.

''Tis a grand day for sailing, Cap'n,' a voice suddenly said. Everyone turned to see Silver approaching from the main deck. He smiled at Amelia. 'You're as trim and as bonnie as a sloop with new sails and a fresh coat o' paint.'

The captain rolled her eyes. 'You can keep that kind of flimflammery for your spaceport floozies, Silver,' she snapped.

'Spaceport floozies! Spaceport floozies!' Morph repeated, mimicking Amelia's voice. Silver quickly covered the little blob with his hat.

'You cut me to the quick, Cap'n,' Silver protested, pretending to be hurt. 'I speaks nothin' but me heart at all times.'

Morph peeked from beneath Silver's hat and mirrored his master's hurt expression. 'Nothin' but me heart,' Morph chimed in.

'By the way, isn't that *your* cabin boy aimlessly footling about in those shrouds?' Amelia said sharply, pointing to Jim.

'A momentary aberration, Cap'n. Soon to be addressed.' Silver turned to Jim and shouted, 'Jimbo! I've got two new friends I'd like ya to meet. Say hello to Mr Mop and Mrs Bucket!' He tossed the cleaning supplies into Jim's hands. Jim looked at them glumly.

'Yippee,' he said.

Chapter 7

A short time later, Jim was listlessly swabbing the aft deck, muttering angrily to himself. Who would've thought sailing could be so *boring*?

Just then a hulking, four-armed alien named Hands came up behind Jim and shoved him into a pile of rigging. 'Watch it, twerp,' the alien growled.

As Hands sauntered away, Jim noticed three other crewmen whispering to each other. He leaned forward, trying to make out what they were saying. The aliens glanced at him and snapped their mouths shut. A broad, muscular alien stepped forward. 'What are you looking at, weirdo?' he barked at Jim. Suddenly, his head crawled off his body! The burly fellow was actually *two* separate aliens – Oxy and Moron!

'Yeah, weirdo!' Moron, the body half of the alien, echoed.

A hissing sound came from above. Jim looked up and saw a large, spidery alien crawling down the rigging towards him. The alien's bug-like yellow eyes glowed with a sinister light.

'Cabin boysss should learn to mind their own businesss,' Scroop, the menacing alien, warned him.

'Why?' Jim retorted quickly. 'You got something to hide, bright eyes?'

In a flash, Scroop grabbed Jim by the collar and pulled him close to his fanged face. 'Maybe your earsss don't work so well!' he threatened.

'Yeah.' Jim coughed and wrinkled his nose. 'Too bad my nose works just fine.'

'Why, you impudent little –' Scroop slammed Jim against a mast. Jim struggled to get free, but the giant spider had him pinned. The crew members crowded round, egging Scroop on.

'Slice him! Dice him!' an alien named Birdbrain Mary called, hopping up and down on her skinny legs.

'Any last wordsss, cabin boy?' Scroop asked, raising his sharp claw to Jim's throat.

Suddenly, a mechanical hand clamped on to Scroop's claw. Jim looked up and saw Silver calmly holding a purp in one hand and Scroop in the other.

'Mr Scroop,' Silver said casually. 'Ya ever see

what happens to a fresh purp when ya squeeze *real* hard?' Silver tightened his grip on Scroop's claw. Scroop winced and released Jim.

'*What's all this, then?*' a stern voice interrupted. Scroop turned to see Arrow approaching.

'You know the rules,' Arrow said. 'There'll be no brawling on this ship!' He glared at the crew. 'Any further offenders will be confined to the brig for the remainder of the voyage. Am I clear, Mr Scroop?' Arrow warned.

'Transparently,' Scroop spat back, seething. Then Silver turned towards Jim, and Scroop skittered up the rigging.

'Jimbo!' Silver boomed. 'I gave you a job to do, and it appears –'

Anger flared in Jim's chest. 'I was doing it until that *bug thing* –'

'*Belay that!*' Silver roared. He picked up the mop and shoved it into Jim's hands. 'Now, I want this deck swabbed spotless, and heaven help ya if I come back and it's not done.' He turned to Morph. 'Keep an eye on this pup an' let me know if there be any more *distractions*,' he instructed.

Morph nodded and flew over to Jim. He transformed into two big eyes and watched as Jim grudgingly picked up the mop and began to swab the deck.

A few moments later, downstairs in the galley, the alien crew members stood sheepishly before Silver. Silver looked them over and nodded curtly. 'So we're all here, then,' he said. The aliens stared at him silently.

'Now,' Silver went on, 'if you'll pardon my plain speakin', gentlemen, are ya all *stark ravin', totally blinkin' DAFT*?' His voice rose to a roar as he paced back and forth. 'After all me finaglin', gettin' us hired as an upstandin' crew, you want to blow the whole mutiny before it's time?' He glared at Scroop, who shifted uneasily.

'The boy wasss sniffing about,' Scroop protested.

'You just stick to the plan, ya bug-brained twit!' Silver growled. His eyes glinted evilly. 'As for the boy, I'll run him so ragged, he won't have time to think!'

Chapter 8

The sun had set by the time Silver returned to the ship's deck. He found Jim finishing up the mopping. Morph had transformed into a mop and was helping him. When Morph saw Silver, he changed back into his normal shape and burped up some bubbles.

Silver whistled at the sight of the clean deck. 'Well, thank heaven for little miracles. You've been up here for an hour and the deck's still in one piece.'

Jim looked up and bit his lip. 'Look . . . What you did . . . Thanks,' he said quietly.

'Didn't your pap ever teach ya to pick your fights a bit more carefully?' Silver asked.

Jim flinched and said nothing.

'Your father's not the teachin' sort?' Silver prompted.

'No, he never got around to that,' Jim said flatly. He walked away and leaned over the ship's rail, looking out at the etherium.

Something in Jim's expression told Silver he'd touched a nerve. 'Ahh, sorry, lad,' he said awkwardly, joining Jim at the rail.

But Jim shook his head. 'Hey, no big deal,' he said, his voice edged with fury. 'I'm doing just fine.'

Silver looked at Jim's sullen face, shifting his weight uncomfortably. There was something about this boy that reminded Silver of himself at a young age, and something in his expression that spoke of pain and loss. And Silver knew that the best antidote for pain was *work*. 'Well,' he said loudly. 'Since the cap'n has put you in *my* charge, like it or not, I'll be poundin' a few skills into that thick head o' yours ta keep you outta trouble.'

'What?' Jim whirled round and stared at him.

Silver nodded. 'From now on, I'm not lettin' you outta me sight,' he continued. 'You won't so much as eat, sleep or scratch your bum without my say-so!'

'Hey, don't do me any favours,' Jim snapped.

Silver chuckled. 'Oh, you can be sure o' that, my lad,' he said confidently. 'You can be sure o' that.'

Silver kept his word. He put Jim to work cleaning out the cannons, scrubbing barnacles from the hull, peeling yelatos in the galley and, of course, swabbing the deck. If he missed so much as a single spot, Silver would make him wash the entire deck again. Every night Jim fell into bed so exhausted he could barely take off his boots, and every morning he rose dreading another day of hard work. The adventures he'd dreamed of before coming aboard the galleon seemed a distant memory.

The weeks passed, and slowly Jim began to find that the work Silver gave him wasn't as difficult as it first had been. He discovered that he could mop the entire aft deck without ever stopping to rest, and he could peel a pile of yelatos the size of a bullyadous without wasting a scrap. The more Silver piled on the work, the more determined Jim became to do it well.

One evening, Silver gave him an entire galley's worth of dirty dishes to clean. Rather than grumbling, as he once would have done, Jim set his jaw and scrubbed until his knuckles were raw. A few hours later, Silver found him asleep on the

galley floor. Silver was about to demand that Jim
get back to work when he realized that the cabin
boy had cleaned and dried every last pot – and
finished in half the time it would have taken any
other sailor! Impressed, Silver covered Jim with
his own coat and let him sleep for the rest of the
night.

Another time, as Jim sat alone in the galley, he
overheard voices on the other side of the wall. He
looked round the corner and saw Silver
entertaining the rest of the crew with an
adventurous tale. He watched the group laughing
at the cyborg's antics and felt a pang of loneliness.
Could it be that he'd misjudged Silver? It didn't
seem possible that Silver, with his hearty laugh
and twinkling eye, could be the cyborg Billy Bones
had warned him about. Little by little, Jim stopped
resenting Silver, and even began to admire him.
The cyborg wasn't mean, Jim thought, he was just
tough, like any spacer had to be. Like his own
father might have been.

For his part, Silver was pleased to see the
change in Jim. The boy worked harder than any
other crew member – so hard, in fact, that Silver
sometimes had trouble coming up with enough
tasks to keep him busy. He showed Jim how to tie

the strongest spacer's knots, and Jim proved to be a whiz. Silver had only to show him the knot once, and Jim could copy it in a flash. Silver had to admit he was starting to admire the boy. Silver had been like Jim once, back before his pirating days, when he still had two normal hands and legs. Back before he'd ever heard about the treasure or Captain Flint.

One day, Jim helped Silver ready a longboat to go sailing in the etherium. Jim steadied the boat as Silver climbed aboard; then, with a wave of his hand, the cyborg set off from the ship. In a flash, Jim recalled the day, many years before, when his father had left Montressor. Jim had been asleep in bed when he'd heard the front door slam. He hurried out to the sitting room and saw his mother slumped at the table, crying. That was when he knew his father was gone. Jim chased after him, calling out to him and running as fast as his nine-year-old legs would go. Jim was sure his father heard him, but he never once turned round. Jim reached the dock just seconds after his father's ship set sail. That was the last time Jim had ever seen him. Now Jim stood in the bay, trying to swallow a lump in his throat as he watched Silver sail off without him – just like his father had.

Almost as though he sensed what Jim was feeling, Silver glanced over his shoulder. To Jim's surprise, Silver turned the longboat round and came back for him. Silver tried to show Jim how to steer the boat. But the old cyborg's jaw dropped in amazement when Jim took the helm confidently, showing off his solar-surfer moves. Silver held on tight as Jim steered the longboat right into the tail of a streaking comet. Jim followed the comet as it looped around, then dropped back out into the calm air, laughing and brushing comet dust from his shoulders. Jim, Silver and Morph spent the rest of the afternoon chasing comets through the etherium.

It was dark by the time they returned to the *Legacy*. They were both laughing as they hauled the longboat up into the ship's hangar bay. 'Ah, Jimbo,' Silver chuckled happily as he stepped into the docked boat and leaned back comfortably. 'If I had manoeuvered a skiff like that when I was your age, they'd be bowin' in the streets when I walked by today.'

'Bowin' in the streets,' Morph chirped.

'I don't know,' Jim said as he joined Silver in the longboat, which swayed gently on its moorings with the motion of the *Legacy*. 'They weren't exactly singing my praises when I left home.' For a moment, they sat quietly in the longboat. Jim's brow furrowed in thought. 'But I'm going to change all that,' he said finally.

'Are ya, now?' Silver asked, stiffening with wariness. 'How so?'

Jim smiled softly. 'I've got some plans that are gonna make people see me a little different.'

Silver gave Jim a sidelong glance. He knew Jim was talking about Treasure Planet – and the riches that Silver himself planned to steal. 'Sometimes plans go astray,' he told Jim uneasily.

Jim placed his hands behind his head confidently. 'Uh-uh,' he said. 'Not this time.'

For the first time in all his years of pirating, Silver felt a pang of guilt. Confused, he leaned over and tried to adjust a bolt on his mechanical leg, which had become stiff during their ride. Morph quickly turned into a wrench and helped him. 'Ah. Thank you, Morphy,' Silver said.

Jim eyed Silver's leg. 'So,' he asked hesitantly, 'how'd that happen, anyway?'

Silver smiled wryly. 'You give up a few things, chasin' a dream.'

Jim raised his eyebrows. 'Was it worth it?'

Silver placed his heavy arm around the boy's

shoulders. 'I'm hopin' it is, Jimbo,' he answered. 'I most surely am.'

Chapter 9

Wham! Suddenly the *Legacy* jolted, and Jim and Silver were thrown forward in the longboat. Morph smacked against the boat's railing. He shattered into tiny pieces, then quickly came back together.

'What the devil?' Silver cried. There was a bright flash of light, and the ship lurched again, throwing everyone off balance.

Jim and Silver hurried to the top deck, and Jim's mouth dropped open at what he saw. Far ahead, the cosmos swirled with the dazzling red light of a thousand furious sunsets. A red dwarf star was radiating streams of brilliant energy, sending star matter hurtling towards the ship. It was beautiful and horrifying all at once.

'Good heavens!' Doppler cried. 'The star Pellucid! It's gone supernova!'

'All hands, fasten your lifelines!' Arrow commanded. The crew hurriedly connected cables to their belts, tying themselves to the mainmast of the ship as another massive energy blast washed over them, sending ship and crew reeling.

'Mr Arrow, secure those sails,' Amelia ordered.

'*Secure all sails. Brace 'em down, men!*' Arrow shouted. Arrow, Scroop and the rest of the crew scrambled up the rigging and began to tie down the sails, which were already tattered from where the energy had blasted through them.

As Jim and Silver tied the jib sail, shards of star matter flew past their heads. *Wham!* A hunk of rock knocked Silver from the mast.

'Silver!' Jim cried in panic as the cyborg tumbled away from the ship and out into space. Suddenly Silver lurched to an abrupt halt as his lifeline pulled taut. Silver was heavy, but Jim's work on the ship had made him strong – and he would not let the cyborg go. Using all his strength, Jim hauled on Silver's lifeline and pulled him back.

'Thanks, lad,' Silver said with a gasp. At that moment, out of the corner of his eye, Jim saw something flying towards them. He turned in time to see a giantic star shard headed straight for the ship. It was enormous – the size of twenty Benbow Inns. There was no time to duck. The shard was going to crush the *Legacy*!

Jim felt his stomach drop as he braced himself for the impact. The enormous shard rolled on, then ... stopped. Jim hardly dared to breathe as it hovered in the air for a split second, then slowly began to move away from the ship! Jim and Silver watched it in wonder. What was happening? They were safe ... but why?

Up in the crow's nest, Onus turned pale. 'Capteen, the star!' he cried. Amelia and Doppler turned to look. The swirling light was starting to spiral into a deep black abyss.

Doppler gasped. 'It's devolving into a ... black hole!' All the destructive matter that had been flying towards the ship was getting sucked backward into the vortex – and the ship was getting pulled in with it. Once they were trapped in the gravitational pull of the black hole, there would be no escape.

On the bridge, the ship's wheel wrenched out of Turnbuckle's grip. 'I cannot hold her, Cap'n!' he cried. Amelia grabbed hold of the wheel, fighting to control it with every ounce of her strength.

'Oh, no, you don't,' Amelia growled. She

grappled with the wheel as the ship was drawn like a magnet towards the expanding cosmic whirlpool. One after another, powerful energy waves washed over them.

Amelia's mind worked frantically. She had never lost a crew member and she wasn't about to lose any now. But how was she going to pull the *Legacy* out of this? As she struggled, another energy wave washed over the ship, twisting the wheel from her hands.

'Blast these waves!' Amelia cried. 'They're so deucedly erratic!'

'No, Captain! They're not erratic at all!' Doppler corrected her, gazing down at the ship's instruments. 'There'll be one more in precisely forty-seven point two seconds, followed by the biggest megillah of them all!'

Amelia frowned as she processed what the professor had just said. If they knew when the energy wave was coming, then they could be ready for it. And maybe they could even make the blast work for them! 'Of course!' she cried. She turned to Doppler, her face lit up with excitement. 'Brilliant, Doctor! We'll ride that last megillah out of here!'

'All sails secured, Captain!' Arrow reported.

'Good man,' Amelia said. 'Now release them immediately!'

Arrow stared at her a moment, then nodded. He'd been in many tight spots with her before, and she'd always managed to get them out alive. 'You heard her, men, unfurl those sails!'

The confused crew climbed back up the masts and began to untie the ropes.

'Mr Hawkins!' Amelia shouted to Jim. 'Make sure all lifelines are secured good and tight!'

'Aye, aye, Captain!' Jim raced to the mainmast. He checked each line carefully, securing them with the sheepshank knot Silver had taught him. Taking his cue from Jim, Morph transformed into a rope and tied himself to the railing.

'Lifelines secured, Captain!' Jim called back confidently, just as the first energy wave engulfed the ship. The *Legacy* was knocked sideways in the enormous blast. Atop the mainmast, Arrow lost his grip and flew into space. But Jim's knot held fast, and he jolted to a stop, hovering in the etherium.

As Arrow began to pull himself back towards the ship, he saw Scroop standing below, on the spar where his lifeline had snagged. Relieved, Arrow reached out a hand. But Scroop made no move to help. In a flash, Scroop swung his spidery arm and slashed through Arrow's lifeline with his claw. The storm's howl drowned out Arrow's scream as he was sucked into the black abyss.

Scroop smiled evilly at the brilliant simplicity of what he'd done. Best of all, there had been no witnesses.

'Captain!' Doppler called out. 'The last wave! Here it comes!'

'Hold on to your lifelines, gents!' Amelia called. 'It's going to be a bumpy ride.' The crew braced themselves. Silver clung to the mainmast, using his body to shield Jim as the ship neared the edge of the black hole. Before them lay only swirling darkness.

Suddenly the etherium lit up with the fire of the last colossal energy wave. The *Legacy* tore away from the black hole, carried by the devastating blast. As the ship raced across the galaxy, Jim held on tight, thinking that the ride would be thrilling if it weren't so terrifying. Battered but still in one piece, the *Legacy* washed up in the sheltering atmosphere of the nearby planet Xenuse.

The stunned crew lay panting on the deck. Then, one by one, they slowly began to pick themselves up. Doppler felt his arms and legs, checking to make sure he was still in one piece. 'She did it!' he shouted. 'That yowling feline *did* it!'

The crew cheered as Doppler rushed to Amelia's side.

'Captain,' Doppler said breathlessly. 'That . . . oh my goodness! That was absolutely . . . That was the most . . .'

Amelia dismissed him with a wave of her hand. 'Oh, tish tosh,' she snorted. 'Actually, Doctor, your astronomical advice was most helpful.'

Doppler's eyes opened wide. A compliment from the captain? 'Well, I have a lot of help to offer anatomically . . . er . . . anamomically . . . ast-astronomically,' he stuttered.

Amelia ignored him and turned to Jim and Silver. 'I must congratulate you, Mr Silver,' she said. 'It seems your cabin boy did a bang-up job with those lifelines.'

Silver nudged Jim, who beamed.

'All hands accounted for, Mr Arrow?' asked Amelia. But there was no response. She turned around. 'Mr Arrow?'

Suddenly Scroop emerged from the shadows. Arrow's hat dangled from his claw. 'I'm afraid Mr

Arrow has been lossst,' Scroop said, staring at Jim. 'Hisss lifeline wass not ssecure.'

Chapter 10

All eyes turned to Jim. 'No!' he cried. 'I checked them all!' He dashed over to the mast to check the lines. His stomach lurched when he saw that one was conspicuously missing. 'They were secure, I swear,' he said. He turned to look at the captain and shrank before her cold stare.

It took a moment for the reality of the situation to sink in. Finally, Amelia spoke. 'Mr Arrow was a fine spacer . . .' The captain stopped to clear her throat. 'Finer than most of us could ever hope to be.' She paused again, and the crew watched her silently. 'But he knew the risks, as do we all. Resume your posts. We carry on.' With her final command, she turned and slowly climbed the stairs to her quarters.

The other crew members glared at Jim, then turned and walked away. Silver looked after him, then glanced up to the spar, where Scroop was toying with the remains of Arrow's lifeline. In a flash, Silver realized what had happened.

Alone on the rigging, Jim stared out at a sea of stars. The solar breeze had quietened, and now the sails barely stirred. Holding a small piece of rope, Jim tied and retied the sheepshank knot. Silver came and stood next to him.

'It weren't your fault, ya know,' he said.

Jim continued to fiddle with the rope, but said nothing. Tears welled in his eyes, and his chest felt tight.

Silver told him, 'Why, half the crew would be spinnin' in that black abyss if not for –'

Jim whirled round. 'Look, don't you get it?' he shouted angrily. 'I screwed up! For two seconds I thought that maybe I could do something right, but . . . I just . . . Just forget it. Forget it.' Embarrassed, he turned away.

But Silver grabbed Jim and looked him straight in the eye. 'Now you listen to me, James Hawkins!' he said. 'You got the makin's of *greatness* in ya! But ya gotta take the helm and chart yer own course. Stick to it, no matter the squalls. And when the time comes ya get the chance to really test the cut o' yer sails and show what yer made of ... well, I hope I'm there catchin' some o' the light coming off o' ya that day!'

Jim stared at him for a moment, then collapsed against Silver's massive chest. Stunned, Silver froze. Then slowly he wrapped his good arm round Jim and patted the boy's head.

'There, there, lad, it's all right,' Silver said awkwardly. He cleared his throat loudly. 'Now, I'd best be gettin' about my watch ... And you'd best be gettin' some shut-eye.'

Jim nodded and started off down the gangway, looking gratefully back over his shoulder at Silver. Troubled and confused, the old cyborg turned away. 'Gettin' intoo deep here, Morphy,' he told his protoplasmic friend. 'Next thing ya know, they'll be sayin' I've gone soft.' He was not aware that Scroop was standing in the shadows, hissing malevolently to himself. He had watched the whole scene.

Chapter 11

Early the next morning, warm shafts of sunlight streamed through the windows of the ship's cabin. Jim was awakened by the stink of a foot dangling from the bunk above him.

'Eew!' he said, swinging his legs out of bed. He put on one of his boots, but when he reached for the other, it scrunched down and hopped away. 'Morph, knock it off,' Jim said, yawning. He bent over to look for the boot – and it came around and kicked him in the behind! Then Morph took off with the real boot.

'Hey, come back here!' Jim cried, chasing after him.

Jim followed Morph into the galley. He lunged at the little shape-shifter and grabbed his boot, but Morph slipped away. Morph ducked in and out of the floor grating, mimicking Jim's frustrated cries.

Then he disappeared. Jim tiptoed around the galley, looking for him. Suddenly, he heard a sound coming from the purp barrel. Jim crept over and looked inside. One of the purps twitched and opened an eye.

'Busted!' Jim said, crawling into the purp barrel after Morph.

Just then, Jim heard footsteps and angry voices muttering. Someone was coming! Before Jim had a chance to climb out of the barrel, the door to the galley swung open.

'What we're saying is, we're gettin' tired of all this waitin'!' Jim heard Birdbrain Mary say.

'There's only three of 'em left,' Hands added.

Jim held his breath and peered through a knothole in the barrel. Birdbrain Mary, Hands, Meltdown and several other crew members were huddled together in a group.

'Ve are vanting to move!' Meltdown shouted.

Suddenly, a cyborg arm came into view. Jim gasped. 'We don't move till we got the treasure map in hand,' Silver growled.

Jim's eyes opened wide. He couldn't believe what he was hearing. So Silver knew about the map? And he was planning a mutiny with the crew!

Jim's mind was still reeling from this discovery when he heard Scroop hiss, 'I sssay we move now!'

Silver's arm shot out. He grabbed Scroop round the neck and lifted him off the ground. 'What's this "I say"?' he roared. 'Disobey my orders again like that stunt ya pulled with Mr Arrow, and so help me you'll be joinin' him!' In the barrel, Jim caught his breath. So Scroop had killed Arrow – and he'd let Jim take the blame!

Silver shoved Scroop, who stumbled backwards, almost knocking over the purp barrel! Jim clung to the sides for dear life, praying the barrel would remain standing. Morph started to squeak, but Jim grabbed him and placed a hand over his mouth.

'Ssstrong talk,' he heard Scroop say, 'but I know otherwise.' Silver and Scroop glared at each other. Without taking his eyes off Silver's, Scroop reached into the purp barrel, groping for a fruit. Jim scrunched down and shoved a purp into Scroop's claw. Jim let his breath out slowly as the claw withdrew.

'You got somethin' ta say, Scroop?' Silver growled.

'It'sss that boy,' Scroop said, slowly examining the purp. 'Methinksss you have a sssoft ssspot for him.' Scroop punctured the fruit with his sharp claw, and purple juice oozed out.

Silver paused, carefully weighing his words. If the crew thought he'd gone soft, they'd turn against him. He couldn't take that chance. 'Now mark me, the lot o' ya,' he said fiercely. 'I care about one thing and one thing only – *Flint's trove*! You think I'd risk it all for the sake o' some nose-wipin' little whelp?'

Jim felt all the air rush out of him, as if he'd just been punched in the stomach. For a moment, he didn't believe Silver was talking about him. Then he heard Scroop say, 'What was it now . . . Oh, "You got the makin'sss of greatnesss in ya –"'

'*Shut yer yap!*' Silver bellowed. 'I cosied up to that kid to keep him off our scent! But I ain't gone soft.'

Jim was crushed. So Silver had never really been his friend after all – he was just using him! His face turned red as his disbelief gave way to hurt, then anger.

Suddenly, they heard Onus, the lookout, yell '*Planet ho!*'

The pirates looked at each other with excitement. Treasure Planet was in sight! Scrambling over one another, they clambered up to the deck, where they saw the green light of the planet shimmering in the distance. They stared, their mouths hanging open.

'Where the devil's me spyglass?' Silver muttered. Realizing he'd left it below decks, he stormed back down the gangway and entered the galley . . . only to discover Jim rushing up to the deck!

The two eyed each other. For a moment, neither spoke.

'Playin' games, are we?' Silver asked finally, trying to determine how much Jim had heard.

'Yeah,' Jim replied angrily. 'We're playin' games.'

'Well, I was never much good at games,' Silver said. Behind his back, his mechanical hand transformed into a pistol. 'Always hated to lose.'

'Mmm,' Jim said, reaching behind him. His hand landed on a metal ice-pick. 'Me too!' He lunged forward, jamming the pick into Silver's cyborg leg. Sparks flew from the leg, which vibrated and locked. Jim tore up the gangway with Morph on his heels.

'Blast it all!' Silver growled as he limped on to the deck. He pulled a whistle from his pocket and blew a shrill note. 'Change of plan, lads!' he shouted to the crew. 'We move now!'

With a tremendous roar, the pirates hurtled down the rigging and barrelled up the gangway.

'Strike her colours, Mr Onus,' Silver commanded.

'Veet pleazure, Capteen!' Onus replied as he lowered the *Legacy*'s flag. In its place he raised a black pirate flag with a three-eyed skull and swirling atoms.

In the captain's stateroom, Amelia hurried to her gun cupboard. 'Pirates on my ship!' she exclaimed. 'I'll see they all hang!' She unlocked the cupboard and tossed a laser flintlock to Doppler. 'Familiar with these?' she asked.

'I've seen . . . uh, well, I've read . . . ' Doppler stammered. Suddenly, the flintlock went off in his hand, shattering a globe. 'No! No, I'm not!' he admitted. Amelia rolled her eyes, then removed the treasure map from the cupboard and tossed it to Jim.

'Mr Hawkins, defend this with your life,' she told him. But before Jim could catch it, Morph swiped it out of the air. Playfully, he dodged Jim's desperate attempts to catch him. 'Gimme that!' Jim cried, at last grabbing the map.

At that moment, laser shots rang around the

door. 'Are ya takin' all day about it?' Silver asked as he pulled a cannon from a compartment in his leg and blasted open the door. The band of pirates burst into the stateroom – only to find an empty room with a hole burned right through the middle of the floor. Jim, Doppler and Amelia had escaped!

Chapter 12

'To the longboats!' Amelia cried as they raced down the gangway. In the ship's hangar bay, she pulled the lever to launch a longboat. As the hatch opened, they leaped into a boat.

But just then, Morph poked into Jim's pocket and pulled out the map. He playfully flew away, wanting Jim to chase him again.

'Morph, *no*!' Jim cried, running after him.

The pirates burst into the bay, firing their weapons.

'Chew on this, you pus-filled boils,' Amelia cried as she and Doppler fired back. Doppler shot out a rivet holding up a metal beam. The beam crashed down, pinning several pirates beneath it.

Amelia's jaw dropped. 'Did you actually aim for that?' she asked.

'You know, I actually did!' Doppler said in

amazement. Together they returned the pirates' laser fire. Suddenly, Silver pulled the lever to close the hangar doors.

'Oh, blast!' cried Amelia, thinking fast. 'Doctor, when I say "Now", shoot out the forward cable. I'll take this one,' she instructed. Doppler nodded and took aim.

Meanwhile, Jim was still trying to get the map from Morph. Realizing that Morph held the map, Silver whistled for his pet.

'Come here, boy!' he called.

'Morph, over here!' Jim cried. Morph looked from one to the other, uncertain which way to go. Suddenly, he dived into a large coil of rope. Jim and Silver dashed forward – but Jim got there first! He retrieved the map and made a break for the longboat.

'Now!' Amelia cried. Doppler and Amelia fired and the cables snapped, launching the boat. Jim took a flying leap and clung to the boat's side. As Doppler pulled him in, Amelia let out the sails. The longboat soared away from the *Legacy*.

Meltdown took aim with the ship's laser cannon. 'Hold your fire! We'll lose the map!' Silver shouted, but it was too late. The cannon fired, sending a laser ball rocketing towards the fleeing longboat.

'Laser ball at twelve o'clock!' Doppler cried. Amelia tried to steer the boat away, but the laser ripped through the mainsail. The longboat plummeted through space towards the green planet below.

Chapter 13

Amelia clenched her teeth. Her shoulder was badly wounded from the laser ball, but she was determined to steer the longboat down safely. Doppler covered his eyes as they crash-landed in a forest of helium trees. The tranquil silence of the lush green forest was shattered as the boat smashed to pieces on the ground and everyone tumbled out.

'Oh, my goodness,' Doppler moaned, crawling away from the wreckage. 'Next time I say I'm looking for adventure, somebody stop me.'

Amelia rose, wobbling on her feet, and chuckled. 'It's not one of my ... gossamer landings,' she said weakly. Then she collapsed.

Jim and Doppler rushed to her side. 'Oh, don't fuss,' she told them. 'Slight bruising, that's all. Cup of tea and I'll be right as rain.' She clutched her shoulder and grimaced with pain, but managed to steady herself. 'Mr Hawkins, the map, if you please?'

Jim reached into his pocket and pulled out the map. But as he held it out to Amelia, it melted in his hand! In its place sat Morph, grinning happily at Jim.

Jim gaped at him. 'Morph? Where's the map?' he cried. Morph transformed into a miniature version of the rope coil, indicating that he'd left the map on the ship.

'Are you serious?' Jim asked furiously. 'It's back on the ship?'

Just then, they heard the sound of another longboat. 'Stifle that blob and get low,' Amelia instructed. 'We've got company.'

They crouched lower as a longboat holding Silver and several pirates cruised overhead. As soon as the boat had passed, Amelia sat up, wincing. 'We need a more defensible position,' she said, handing a flintlock to Jim. 'Mr Hawkins, scout ahead.'

'Aye, Captain,' Jim replied. While Doppler looked after Amelia, Jim set off into the forest with Morph trailing behind him.

Jim and Morph made their way through a dense jungle of giant ferns and mushroom-like plants. The silence around them was almost absolute, and Jim strained to hear whether anyone was following them. They had not gone far when suddenly they heard a rustling in some nearby bushes. Jim looked back, but nothing was there.

As they continued, Jim again heard the rustling sound. He looked back over his shoulder, but saw nothing. 'Shh!' he said to Morph, ducking down in the bushes. Jim gripped his laser, pulled aside a branch . . . and found himself face to face with a pair of huge yellow eyes!

Before Jim could react, something leaped out of the bushes, knocking him backwards! Jim and the thing rolled across the ground. When they came to a stop, Jim found himself in the grip of a rickety robot with skinny limbs and telescopic eyes.

'Oooh!' the robot squealed. 'This is fantastic! A carbon-based life-form come to rescue me at last!' He grabbed Jim's knees and hugged them. 'I just wanna hug ya and squeeze ya and hold ya close to me!'

'Just let go of me!' Jim said, pushing the robot away.

'Oh, sorry, sorry!' the robot said. 'It's just, I've been marooned here for so long. I mean, solitude's fun, don't get me wrong, but after a hundred years *ya go a little nuts*!'

Sensing Jim's alarm, he made an effort to calm down. 'I'm sorry . . . My name is . . .' The robot paused, unable to remember. Morph glanced at Jim and made a cuckoo noise.

'B.E.N.!' the robot suddenly remembered. 'I'm B.E.N.! Bio-Electronic Navigator! And you are . . . ?'

'Jim.'

'Pleasure to meet ya, Jimmy,' B.E.N. said, pumping Jim's hand.

'It's *Jim,*' Jim corrected him. 'Look, I'm kind of in a hurry. I've gotta find a place to hide. There are pirates chasing me and –'

'Oh, *pirates*! Don't get me started on pirates,' B.E.N. said chattily. 'I don't like them!' Jim rolled his eyes and had started to walk away when suddenly he heard the robot say, 'I remember Captain Flint! This guy had such a temper!' Jim spun round and hurried back to B.E.N.

'Wait! You know Captain Flint?' he asked excitedly.

'I think he suffered from mood swings, personally,' B.E.N. went on. 'I'm not a therapist, but –'

'But then you gotta know about the treasure!' Jim interrupted.

'Treasure?' B.E.N. looked at him blankly.

'Yeah,' Jim said. 'Flint's trove. You know... the loot of a thousand worlds?'

'Well, it's all a little fuzzy,' B.E.N. admitted. He grabbed his head, thinking hard. 'Wait! I remember treasure ... lots of treasure buried in the centroid of the mechanism ... and there was this big door opening and closing...' As B.E.N. concentrated, he began to twitch. The little robot was overloading his memory banks! '... and opening and closing ... and Captain Flint wanted to make sure *nobody* could *ever* get to his treasure, so I helped him ... I helped him ...' Suddenly, sparks started to fly from the robot's head. '*Data inaccessible! Reboot! Reboot!*' he cried.

Jim slapped him hard. The robot quietened and looked around. He stared at Jim. 'And you are ...?' he asked.

'Wait! Wait! What about the treasure?' Jim cried.

'I wanna say Larry,' the robot guessed. He

shook his head. 'I'm sorry, my memory isn't what it used to be. I've lost my mind.' B.E.N. looked at Jim thoughtfully. 'You haven't found it, have you?'

'What?' Jim asked.

'My missing piece? My primary memory circuit?' B.E.N. pointed to an oddly shaped hole in his head.

Realizing the robot couldn't help them, Jim turned away. 'Look, B.E.N.,' he said. 'I really need to find a place to hide. So I'm just going to be . . . you know . . . moving on.'

'Oh.' B.E.N. blinked sadly. 'So, I guess this is goodbye, huh?' He turned and slowly walked away, dragging his feet. Jim glanced guiltily at Morph and sighed.

'Look,' he called after the robot. 'If you're gonna come along, you're going to have to stop talking.'

B.E.N.'s face lit up. 'This is fantastic!' he shouted. 'Me and my best buddy out looking for a –' Jim gave him a warning look. 'Sorry . . . sorry, being quiet,' B.E.N. finished sheepishly.

Jim nodded. 'Now, I think we should –'

'Say, listen,' the robot interrupted. 'Before we go out on our *big search,* would you mind if we make a quick pit stop at my place? Kind of urgent.' B.E.N. parted some branches. There on a hill stood a tower, overgrown with vines.

Jim smiled. 'B.E.N., I think you just solved my problem.'

Chapter 14

A short time later, Jim pushed open the entrance of B.E.N.'s tower. Doppler followed, carrying the wounded Amelia.

'Pardon the mess, people!' B.E.N. called as they came through the door. 'You'd think in a hundred years I would've dusted a little more often.' He sighed when he noticed Doppler and Amelia. 'Ah, isn't that sweet,' he said, mistaking them for newly-weds. 'I find old-fashioned romance so touching. How about drinks for the happy couple?' He bustled over, holding a tray of cups filled with mechanical oil.

Doppler gently set Amelia down. 'Oh, no, we don't drink,' he said, then quickly added, 'And we're not a couple.' He looked around at the walls of the room. 'Look at these markings!' he exclaimed. 'They're identical to the ones on the map. I suspect these are the hieroglyphic remnants of an ancient culture.'

But Amelia was more concerned with the pirates. 'Mr Hawkins! Halt anyone who tries to approach,' she ordered, then grimaced with pain. Doppler knelt next to her and gave her a worried look. He folded his coat into a pillow and gently placed it under her head.

'Now listen to me. Stop giving orders for a few milliseconds and lie still!' he said.

Amelia smiled weakly. 'Very forceful, Doctor. Go on . . . say something else.' Doppler smiled back at her.

Just then, B.E.N. looked out the door. 'Hey, look! There's some more of your buddies. Hey, fellas! We're over here!' he called, waving.

At the sound of B.E.N.'s voice, the group of pirates headed for the tower and began firing their weapons. Jim pulled B.E.N. down and fired back.

Suddenly, Jim heard Silver call, 'Halloo, up there!' Jim peered out. Silver was standing in a clearing, waving a white shirt like a flag. 'Jimbo,' he shouted. 'If it's all right with the cap'n, I'd like a short word with ya. No tricks,' he promised.

Jim looked at Amelia. She frowned. 'Come to bargain for the map, no doubt,' she growled. But her mouth clamped shut as a wave of pain washed over her.

'Captain!' Doppler cried with concern.

But Jim brightened. 'That means that he thinks we still have it!' He hurried out of the tower, down to meet Silver. Morph followed.

'Ah, Morphy,' Silver said as they approached. 'I wondered where you lit off to.' Morph happily nuzzled his cyborg friend.

Silver sat down on a rock and adjusted his metal leg. 'This poor old leg's been downright snarky since that game o' tag we had in the galley,' he said, winking at Jim. Jim stared back at him, unsmiling.

'Whatever you heard back there – at least the part concernin' you – I didn't mean a word of it,' Silver told him. 'If that bloodthirsty lot had thought I'd gone soft, they'd of gutted us both.' Jim glared at Silver. The cyborg leaned closer, whispering, 'If we play our cards right, we can both walk away from this rich as kings.'

'Yeah?' Jim said cautiously.

'You get me that map, and an even portion of the treasure is yours,' Silver promised. He held out his hand, smiling hopefully.

Jim grinned without humour. 'Boy, you are

really something!' he said. Then he laughed bitterly and his smile disappeared. 'All that talk of greatness, light comin' off my sails. What a joke!'

Silver's smile faded, and a look of regret flashed across his face. 'Now see here, Jimbo –' he began.

'I mean, at least you taught me one thing,' Jim went on. 'Stick to it, right? Well, that's just what I'm gonna do. I'm gonna make sure that you never see one dubloon of *my* treasure!'

Silver's face flushed with anger. 'That treasure is owed *me,* by thunder!' he shouted.

'Well, try to find it without my map, *by thunder*!' Jim retorted.

Silver drew himself up to his full height. 'You still don't know how to pick your fights, do ya, boy?' he said threateningly. 'Now mark me, either I get that map by dawn tomorrow, or so help me . . . *I'll use the ship's cannons to BLAST YA ALL TO KINGDOM COME!*' Silver roared so fiercely that even Morph was frightened. He flew to Jim's side, which only increased Silver's rage.

'Morph, hop to it!' Silver commanded, pointing to his shoulder. But the terrified Morph stayed put. '*Now!*' Silver's mechanical eye glowed red with fury. Morph cowered and hid behind Jim.

With a wave of his hand, Silver stormed off. But a few paces away, he turned and looked back over his shoulder. His face fell as he watched Jim and Morph, the only two friends he'd ever had, walk away.

Chapter 15

Back in B.E.N.'s tower, Jim told Doppler and the half-conscious Amelia what had happened. 'Gentlemen, we must stay together,' Amelia said woozily. 'And . . . and . . .' Her eyes drifted closed.

'And what?' cried Doppler.

Amelia's eyes opened slowly, and she gazed at Doppler. 'Doctor,' she said. 'You have . . . wonderful eyes . . .'

'*She's lost her mind!*' Doppler shouted.

'Well, you gotta *help* her!' Jim told him.

'Dang it, Jim!' Doppler cried. 'I'm an astronomer, not a doctor. I mean, I am a doctor, but I'm not *that* kind of doctor. I have a doctorate – it's not the same thing. You can't help people with a doctorate. You just sit there and you're useless!' He clutched his head in despair. Jim grabbed his shoulders, trying to calm him down.

'It's OK, Doc. It's all right,' Jim said.

'Yeah, Doc. Jimmy knows exactly how to get out of this,' B.E.N. chimed in. He turned to Jim and whispered, 'Any thoughts at all?'

Jim shook his head. 'Without the map, we're dead!' he said. 'If we try to leave, we're dead! If we stay –'

'*We're dead!*' Morph piped up, imitating the sound of Jim's voice. '*We're dead! We're dead! We're dead!*'

Jim stared out the window at the setting sun.

B.E.N. looked at him nervously. 'Well, I think that Jimmy could use a little quiet time,' he said. 'So I'll just slip out the back door . . .'

'Back door?' Jim looked up. B.E.N. was rotating a metallic sphere on the floor.

'Oh, yeah,' he told Jim. 'I get this delightful breeze through here.' Jim darted over and helped the robot open the vent. A gust of cool air blew through the tunnel. Peering down, Jim saw a vast network of underground machinery.

'What is all that stuff?' Jim asked.

'You mean the miles and miles of machinery that run through the entire course of the inside of this planet?' BEN shrugged. 'Not a clue!'

'Hey, Doc,' Jim called. 'I think I found a way out of here!'

'No, Jim, wait!' Doppler cried. 'The captain ordered us to stay together!'

But Jim had already made up his mind. 'I'll be back!' he said, and disappeared down the passageway. Morph followed him. B.E.N. waved at Doppler, then jumped in after them. '*Cannonball!*' he cried as he fell.

Doppler shook his head as he stared after them unhappily.

The secret tunnel ended at a large metal grate covered with brambles and vines. It creaked as Jim cautiously pushed it open and peered outside. Not far away, he could see Silver, Turnbuckle, Birdbrain Mary and Meltdown snoring round a campfire. Jim took a few quiet steps. Suddenly, B.E.N. popped up in front of him. 'So what's the plan?' he asked loudly.

Jim nearly jumped out of his shoes. 'Shhh! B.E.N.! Quiet!' he whispered urgently. He clamped his hand over B.E.N.'s mouth. Silver stirred, but didn't wake.

'OK,' Jim whispered. 'We sneak back to the

Legacy, disable the laser cannons and bring back the map!'

'That's a good plan,' B.E.N. mumbled through Jim's fingers. 'The only thing is . . . how do we get there?'

Jim smiled. 'On that,' he said, pointing to the pirates' longboat which hovered in the air, tied to a nearby tree.

Chapter 16

Moments later Jim, Morph and B.E.N. sailed up to the *Legacy*. They peeked over the rail to see if the coast was clear, then crept aboard the ship. B.E.N. stumbled over the rail, his metal limbs clattering on the deck.

'B.E.N., shhh!' Jim whispered urgently.

'Sorry, sorry,' B.E.N. said.

They quietly made their way down to the lower deck.

'OK,' Jim whispered. 'I'll get the map. You wait here.'

'Roger, Jimmy! I'll neutralize the laser cannons, sir!' Before Jim could stop him, B.E.N. took off in search of the control room, singing, 'Yo-ho, yo-ho! A pirate's life for me . . .'

Jim hurried to the hangar bay and found the coil of rope that Morph had dropped the map into.

'Yes!' he cried with relief as his hand closed round the familiar sphere.

Meanwhile, B.E.N. had found the control room. 'Disable a few laser cannons. What's the big deal?' he said to himself. 'All we gotta do is find that one little wire.' He opened a control box and looked at the jumble of wires inside. Choosing a random wire, he disconnected it. A siren blared through the ship.

'Bad B.E.N.,' the robot scolded himself. He reconnected the wire and continued to poke through the box.

Hearing the siren, Jim frantically began searching for B.E.N. 'That stupid robot's gonna get us all killed,' he muttered to Morph. Jim and Morph ran up the gangway – only to find Scroop blocking their path!

'Cabin boy,' Scroop growled. Jim turned and ran back the way he'd come, with Scroop hot on his heels. As he ran, Jim knocked over barrels, trying to block Scroop's path, but the spidery alien only crawled on to the ceiling. Scroop was bearing down on Jim when Morph suddenly turned into a pie and threw himself at Scroop's face.

'Get off!' Scroop snarled. He shoved Morph away and chased after Jim.

Rounding a corner, Jim pulled out his laser flintlock. He could see Scroop coming towards him. Jim raised the pistol and took aim –

Suddenly, the room went dark! In the control room, B.E.N. had disconnected another wire.

The emergency lights came on, bathing the room in eerie red light. Scroop was gone! Jim turned to look behind him, laser gun cocked, but Scroop was nowhere in sight.

Jim slowly backed down the hallway, unaware of the dark, spidery shadow looming behind him. Just then, Morph burst from a pipe and screamed when he saw Scroop. Jim spun round. *Wham!* Scroop knocked him to the ground. Jim's laser flintlock flew from his hand. Scroop leaped on top of Jim, pressing his claw to Jim's throat.

In the next moment, Jim and Scroop found themselves floating in mid-air! B.E.N. had accidentally deactivated the gravity! Jim kicked Scroop away with such force that the alien crashed through a window. Jim sailed out behind him.

Jim and Scroop rose up above the deck. Scroop grabbed the mainmast, then swiped at Jim as he flew past. Jim made a desperate grab for the pirate flag to keep from flying into space. His laser gun drifted past him. He stretched out a hand but couldn't reach it.

'Oh, no!' he cried.

'Oh, yesss,' said Scroop. He raised his claw and began to saw through the rope that held the pirate flag. Then he turned back to Jim. Just as Scroop lunged at him, Jim leaped and managed to grab hold of the wooden mast. Thrown off balance, Scroop had to grab the pirate flag to keep from floating away. *Snap!* The last of the rope holding the flag broke free. Gripping the flag between his claws, Scroop screamed in terror as he was sucked away into space.

Back in the control room, B.E.N. finally managed to reactivate the gravity. Jim tumbled back down to the deck. Suddenly, Morph appeared beside him. A moment later B.E.N. emerged from the control room, triumphant.

'Laser cannons disconnected, Captain Jimmy, sir!' he called. 'See? That wasn't so tough.'

Bruised but still in one piece, Jim picked himself up. He held up his hand, smiling.

The treasure map shone between his fingers.

Chapter 17

The observation deck in B.E.N.'s tower was dark when Jim, Morph and B.E.N. returned from the ship. Jim moved quickly towards a figure slumped against the wall. 'Doc, wake up!' Jim said. 'I got the map!' He held it out to the doctor.

But the hand that reached out to take the map wasn't Doppler's – it was a metal claw!

'Fine work, Jimbo,' Silver said, emerging from the shadows. 'Fine work indeed.'

Jim's eyes darted around the room. In one corner, he saw Doppler and Amelia, bound and gagged. Jim turned to run, but Onus, Turnbuckle, Birdbrain Mary and the other pirates surrounded him.

'Thanks for showing us the way in, boy,' Turnbuckle said with a sneer. Jim couldn't believe it – the pirates had only been pretending to be asleep when he sneaked out of the vent. Jim turned to run, but Meltdown and Turnbuckle grabbed him and pinned his arms. Morph flew over and bit Meltdown's scaly tail, but the pirate swung back, sending Morph flying. Whimpering, Morph slipped into Jim's pocket.

B.E.N. started to creep back down the vent, but Birdbrain Mary caught him. She waved her dagger in his face, crying, 'What's this sorry stack o' metal?'

B.E.N. cowered. 'Not the face!' he pleaded.

'You're just like me, Jimbo,' Silver said, chuckling. 'Ya hates ta lose.' He held up the gleaming map and tried to open it. But it wouldn't budge. Jim smirked as Silver struggled with the map.

At last, Silver shoved the map into Jim's hand. 'Open it!' he demanded.

Jim glared at Silver defiantly. Silver glared back – and transformed his hand into a pistol! 'I'd get busy,' he told Jim.

Jim looked at Doppler and Amelia. Doppler nodded for him to open the map, but Amelia scowled and shook her head. Jim paused for a moment, considering. Then, with a few quick twists, he opened the map. The image of Treasure

Planet glowed in the air before them. As they watched, the smart pixels formed into a corkscrew path that shot out the window. Silver looked out. The path spiralled over the horizon. He chuckled gleefully.

'Tie 'im up and leave 'im with the others,' he said, pointing at Jim. Suddenly, the path disappeared and the room went dark. 'What?' Silver cried. He looked over at Jim, who held the closed map in his hand.

'You want the map, you're takin' me, too,' Jim told him.

Silver looked at him for a few seconds. Then he smiled grudgingly. 'We'll take 'em all,' he said to the pirates.

Chapter 18

The sun was up by the time the pirates' longboat came to a stop near the end of the map's path. Doppler and Amelia, still tied up, stayed on board, guarded by Meltdown. Jim, Silver and the other pirates climbed off the boat. They would go the rest of the way on foot.

As they walked, the frightened Morph stayed in Jim's pocket, while B.E.N. clung to Jim's side. 'Jimmy, I don't know about you, but I'm starting to see my life pass in front of my eyes,' he said.

'B.E.N., shhh,' Jim told him, glancing at Silver. 'This isn't over yet.'

The path led straight into a dense grove of trees and started to glow brilliantly. 'We're gettin' close!' Silver exclaimed. 'I smell treasure a-waitin'!' The pirates whooped and hollered, slicing through the trees with their swords as they went.

But when they emerged from the foliage, all they found was a sheer cliff. The path led right off the edge!

'Where is it?' Oxy demanded.

'I see nuttink!' Onus growled. 'Vun great big steenking hunk of nuttink!'

Suddenly the smart pixels began to swirl. Spiralling through the air, they whooshed back into the map, which snapped shut.

'What's going on, Jimbo?' Silver asked angrily.

'I don't know,' Jim replied. 'I can't get it open!' He struggled with the map, but it wouldn't budge.

'We shoulda never followed this boy,' Birdbrain Mary said, shoving Jim to the ground.

'I'd suggest ya get that gizmo goin' again – and *fast*,' Silver snarled.

The pirates crowded round Jim. 'Throw him over cleef!' Onus shouted.

Just then, Jim noticed a pattern carved into the rocky cliff. The markings were just like the ones on the map! And right in the middle was a small, round hole – exactly the same size as the map. Jim placed the map in the hole. As soon as it clicked into place, the pattern in the rock began to glow. Suddenly, a three-dimensional hologram of the map rose from the rock and floated in the air before Jim. He cautiously stretched out a hand to touch it.

But before his fingers made contact, the ground began to rumble. Three brilliant streams of energy streaked across the floor of the valley below them. The energy beams came together at the base of the cliff, then shot straight up into the sky. There was a blinding flash. Suddenly, a twenty-metre-high triangle opened in the sky before them. The pirates gasped.

Peering into the triangular portal, Jim could feel the breeze of the etherium against his face. Beyond the portal, he saw a spectacular spiral nebula.

Jim recognized it. 'The Lagoon Nebula?' he said in wonder.

'But that's halfway across the galaxy!' Silver cried. Jim looked down at the glowing green holographic map before him. Carefully, he touched a point on it. The portal flashed again and opened on to a shimmering crystal cityscape. He touched another point. This time the portal opened on to the dunes of a barren red desert.

'A big door opening and closing,' Jim said to himself, remembering B.E.N.'s words. Suddenly, Jim had an idea. 'Montressor spaceport,' he said, experimentally touching a crescent-shaped point on the controller. The portal opened on to Crescentia, the port where Jim and Doppler had first boarded the *Legacy*. 'So *that's* how Flint did it! He used this portal to roam the universe, stealing treasure!'

'But where'd he stash it all? Where's that blasted treasure?' Silver cried in frustration. He shoved Jim aside and began touching points on the controller. The portal began to flash rapidly through different locations.

B.E.N. clutched his head. He was trying to remember. 'Treasure . . . buried in the . . .'

'*Buried* in the *centroid* of the *mechanism*!' Jim finished. His memory worked furiously, recalling the miles of machinery that snaked into the centre of the planet below. 'What if the whole planet is the mechanism? Then the treasure is buried in the centre of this planet!'

The pirates snatched up their picks and shovels and began hacking away at the ground. *Clang!* Their tools struck hard metal. They stopped digging and stared dumbly at one another.

'How in blue blazes are we supposed to get there?' Silver asked.

'Just . . . open the right door,' Jim replied. He

reached out and touched a point shaped like Treasure Planet in the very centre of the controller.

With a sudden flash, the portal opened to a dark, silent chamber.

Chapter 19

Jim waved his arm through the portal, testing to see if he could enter the other dimension. Seeing that he could, he walked straight through. The pirates cautiously followed him. Once inside, they came to an abrupt stop. Their eyes opened wide.

Before them lay mountains of treasure as far as the eye could see. Everywhere they turned, they saw gleaming piles of gold, gemstones as big as a man's fist, crystal goblets, valuable paintings, marble statues, golden weapons . . .

'The loot of a thousand worlds,' Silver murmured. He dropped to his knees, mesmerized by the sight. 'A lifetime o' searchin', but at long last . . . I can touch it!' He scooped up a handful of jewels and let them trickle through his mechanical fingers.

'YEEEE-HAAAAA!' The other pirates rushed forward and dived into the treasure. They began frantically to stuff their pockets with gemstones and gold coins.

Jim watched Silver, then looked around the chamber. The treasure covered the entire surface of a gigantic sphere. The sphere itself floated in the centre of Treasure Planet, held in place by columns of energy that rose from huge cannons.

As Jim took in the magnificence of the room, B.E.N. fidgeted nervously. Something was bothering him, but he couldn't remember what. 'This is all seeming very familiar ...' he said slowly.

Just then, Jim spied Flint's treasure-filled ship, which rested atop a pile of gold. 'Come on, B.E.N.,' he whispered. 'We're gettin' outta here, and we're not leaving empty-handed.' He grabbed B.E.N. and pulled him towards the ship.

On the bridge of Flint's ship, Jim worked the rusty throttle, trying to start the engines. B.E.N. looked around.

'There's something that's nagging at the back of my mind,' he told Jim. Suddenly, B.E.N. gasped. 'Captain Flint!' he cried. Jim and B.E.N. were standing before a skeleton seated on an elegant jewelled throne.

'My, you look different,' B.E.N. said to the remains of Captain Flint. As Jim moved towards the throne, B.E.N. continued to fret. 'I remember there was something horrible Flint didn't want anyone else to know, but I can't remember what it was . . .' B.E.N. sighed. 'A mind is a terrible thing to lose.'

Just then, Jim noticed something clenched in Flint's bony fist. He prised apart the skeleton's fingers. In Flint's hand lay B.E.N.'s missing memory chip.

'B.E.N., hold still,' Jim said. 'I think I just found your mind.' Quickly, he inserted the chip into the back of the robot's head. B.E.N. shuddered. Then his eyes focused.

'Whoa! Hello! You know, Jimmy, I was just thinking. All my memories are flooding back! Right up until Flint pulled my memory circuit so I could never tell anybody about his . . . *booby trap*!'

Suddenly, an explosion above them shook the cavern.

'Flint wanted to make sure nobody could ever steal his treasure!' B.E.N. explained. 'So he rigged this whole planet to blow higher than a Callypsian kite!'

A series of explosions shook the cavern as the

energy beams began to fall apart. One broke loose from the ceiling and crashed down into the piles of loot. The fiery blast from another energy cannon tore through the cavern floor. The pirates watched in horror as Flint's treasure began to slide into the giant fissure left in its wake.

B.E.N. grabbed Jim. 'Run, Jimmy!' he screamed. 'Run for your life!'

But Jim stood firm on Flint's loot-filled ship. He had another idea. If he could fly the ship out of there, he'd still have enough treasure to make him rich for life.

'You go back and help the Captain and Doc,' he told B.E.N. 'If I'm not there in five minutes, leave without me!'

'I am not leaving my buddy Jimmy,' B.E.N. said. Jim glared at him. 'Unless he looks at me like that. *Bye, Jim!*' With a wave, the robot darted off.

Explosions shook the cavern as the pirates raced madly back towards the portal. Trying to carry a treasure chest, Turnbuckle and a roper named Pigors tripped and fell shrieking into a crevasse. The other pirates dropped their loot and ran.

'Come back here, ya blighters!' Silver roared, shaking his fist at them.

The treasure was nearly gone, fallen into the deep fissures in the cavern floor. Silver looked around desperately. Suddenly, he heard the sound of an engine firing. He turned and spied Jim climbing to the helm of Flint's ship. The cyborg smiled and started after him.

Chapter 20

Meanwhile, the ground beneath the longboat was shaking violently. But Doppler was so focused on Amelia that he hardly noticed. 'I'm just sorry I couldn't have been ... more helpful to you,' he told her.

'Oh, don't be daft,' Amelia said. She was so weak that her voice was barely a whisper. 'You've been very helpful.'

'I feel like such a useless weakling.' Doppler put his head in his hands. Suddenly he noticed that his wrists were no longer tied. His wrists were so thin that they had slipped right out of the knots!

Doppler looked up and saw the retreating pirates hurrying back to the longboat. He didn't have much time! He turned to the pirate guarding them. 'Excuse me, brutish pirate,' he said.

Meltdown belched.

'Yes, you. I have a question,' said Doppler. Meltdown looked at him. 'Is it that your body is too massive for your teeny tiny head? Or is it that your head is too teeny tiny for your big fat body?'

Meltdown grabbed Doppler and lifted him up. 'I pummel you good!'

'Yes, I'm sure you will. But I have one more question.' Doppler whipped out a laser flintlock and pressed it against Meltdown's stomach. 'Is this yours?'

In the cavern, the engines of Flint's ship roared to life. Jim stood at the wheel, ready to steer the treasure-filled ship to safety.

'Ah, Jimbo! Aren't you the seventh wonder of the universe!' said a voice behind him. Jim spun round. Silver was hobbling towards him, chuckling evilly. Frantically, Jim picked up a gold sword from a nearby chest and pointed it at Silver.

'Get back!' he cried.

But Silver stepped closer. 'I like ya, lad,' he said. 'But I've come too far to let you stand between me and me treasure.' He pressed his chest against the tip of the sword. Jim paused, then lowered the weapon. No matter how badly Jim

107

wanted that treasure, he wasn't ready to hurt Silver to get it.

Wham! The ship lurched hard as a wild energy beam blasted into its stern. Jim and Silver flew across the deck and tumbled over the rail. Silver extended his mechanical arm and managed to catch hold of the bow. He looked up and saw that the ship and all its treasure were being sucked into the fiery energy beam!

'Oh no ya don't!' Silver roared. Using all his strength, he tried to pull the ship out of the beam. Suddenly, Morph flew into Silver's face, trying to get his attention.

'What?' Silver said. Morph pointed. Silver looked down and saw Jim dangling over a giant crack in the cavern floor, clinging desperately to the edge with his fingertips.

'Jimbo!' Silver cried. Straining mightily, he began to haul the ship back towards Jim. But the ship caught on a ledge and wouldn't budge. Unwilling to let his treasure go, Silver extended his mechanical arm towards Jim as far as it would go.

'Reach for me!' he told Jim. But he still wasn't close enough.

Just then, the ledge Jim was holding crumbled. Jim slipped and fell into the crevasse!

'Silver!' he cried. He managed to grab on to another ledge. But now there was no way Silver could reach him without letting go of Flint's ship. For a desperate moment, the cyborg looked back and forth from the treasure to Jim.

'Oh, blast me for a fool!' Silver cursed. He let go of the ship and dashed over to the ledge. Just as Jim fell, Silver caught his hand and pulled him to safety.

The two looked up in time to see the energy beam engulf Flint's ship. Jim and Silver watched, stunned, as the last of Flint's treasure vaporized. Then they scrambled to their feet and raced back towards the portal's opening.

They collapsed, panting, on the cliff.

'Silver,' Jim said breathlessly, between gulps of air. 'You gave up the . . .'

'Just a lifelong obsession, Jim,' Silver said wryly. 'I'll get over it.'

They smiled at each other a moment. But they weren't safe yet. The cliff had cracked away from the surrounding landscape! It could crumble at any moment!

Then the *Legacy* loomed before them. Doppler stood at the helm, with Amelia at his side. B.E.N. waved at them from the bridge, where he sat at the control panel. 'Hurry, people!' he exclaimed. 'We've got exactly two minutes and thirty-four seconds until the planet self-destructs!'

As soon as the ship was close enough, Jim and Silver leaped on board.

'Take us out of here, metal man,' Amelia told B.E.N.

'Aye, Captain!' B.E.N. saluted and activated the ship's thrusters. The ship streaked away as debris from the planet's exploding machinery rained around them like missiles.

Silver gave Amelia a charming smile. 'Oh, Cap'n, you dropped from the heavens in the nick o' –'

'Save your claptrap for the judge, Silver!' she told him.

Suddenly, a piece of exploding debris slammed into the mast and broke off a sail. The falling mast crashed into the laser cannon, crushing it. The ship slowed and began to make a grinding noise.

'Mizzen sails demobilized, Captain!' B.E.N. cried. 'Thrusters at only thirty per cent of capacity!'

'Thirty per cent?' Doppler said. 'That means we'll never clear the planet's explosion in time.' He looked anxiously at Amelia.

Jim raced to the bridge and looked back at the portal. Suddenly, he had an idea!

Chapter 21

'We gotta turn around!' Jim cried. He leaped on to the lower deck and ran towards the cannon debris. 'There's a portal back there that can get us outta here!'

'Pardon me, Jim,' Doppler said. 'But didn't that portal open on to a *raging inferno*?'

'Yes! But I'm gonna change that,' Jim said. 'I'm gonna open a different door.' He started roping together a long piece of metal from the cannon debris and the cannon's energy cylinder.

Doppler turned to Amelia. 'Captain, I really don't see how this could possibly –'

'One minute twenty-nine seconds till the planet's destruction,' B.E.N. reported.

Silver leaped to the ship's rail and used his mechanical eye to zoom in on the portal's controller. Sure enough, it was still intact. '*Listen to the boy!*' he cried. He raced down to the lower deck and began to help Jim. 'What do ya need, Jim?'

'I need to attach this to that,' Jim said, pointing to the cylinders and the scrap of metal. Silver transformed his arm into a blowtorch and quickly welded the pieces together. They'd created a makeshift solar surfer, minus the sail. Silver helped Jim haul it to the rail.

'No matter what happens, keep the ship heading straight for that portal,' Jim instructed.

'*Fifty-eight seconds!*' B.E.N. cried.

Jim kicked the power cylinder into gear and shot off the side of the ship. Silver turned back to Doppler and Amelia. 'Well, you heard him!' he shouted. 'Get this blasted heap turned round!'

Doppler looked at Amelia. She paused, then said, 'Doctor, head us back to the portal!'

'Aye, Captain,' said Doppler. He turned the ship and headed towards the portal as explosions sounded around them.

Meanwhile, Jim had almost reached the controller when he lost power in his first energy cylinder. He kicked the second cylinder into gear and rocketed forward, dodging chunks of exploding debris. The cliff and the triangular portal were just ahead. Through the portal opening, Jim could see the firestorm raging in the treasure chamber.

Jim had almost reached the portal controls when – *kaboooom!* A huge explosion sent pieces of machinery hurtling into his path. Jim zigzagged, dodging the shrapnel.

'*Twenty-five seconds!*' BEN shouted.

Just then, Jim lost power. Frantically, he tried to kick his last cylinder into gear, but it was jammed. No matter how hard he kicked, the cylinder wouldn't engage.

'No . . . no!' Jim shouted as he tumbled through the air into a deep chasm.

With his heart in his throat, Silver watched Jim fall. 'Come on, lad!' he cried frantically.

'*Seventeen seconds!*'

Jim's mind raced. If only he could find some way to start the last cylinder, he'd have just enough power to make it to the portal. Suddenly, he got an idea. Flipping upside down, Jim scraped the edge of his surfer against the chasm wall. The friction created a spark, igniting the energy cylinder. A violent explosion sent Jim rocketing straight up out of the chasm. He was only a few feet away from the portal controller.

'*Seven . . . six . . . five . . . four . . . three . . . two . . .*'
B.E.N. counted down.

At the last second, Jim reached out and touched the crescent-shaped point on the controller. The portal flashed. The ship disappeared through the portal just as Treasure Planet exploded in a massive fireball.

Chapter 22

The *Legacy* burst out of the portal into calm space, trailed by the remains of the exploding planet. Close by, they could see the spaceport Crescentia. But where was Jim? Everyone aboard the ship looked back towards the portal. At that moment, Jim rocketed into view, silhouetted against the blinding explosion from Treasure Planet. A moment later, the portal disappeared. All around them, the etherium was quiet.

'Ha, ha, ha! Glory be!' Silver cheered. 'Ya done it, Jim!' He turned to the rest of the crew. 'Didn't I say the lad had greatness in him?'

Everyone cheered as Jim steered his surfer over to the ship. Even the pirates locked in the ship's stockade whooped and hollered. Overcome with emotion, Doppler and Amelia hugged, then looked at each other with surprise. They both smiled, pleased and embarrassed, then hurried to help Jim aboard.

'Unorthodox, but ludicrously effective,' Amelia congratulated Jim as he landed lightly on deck. 'I'd be proud to recommend you to the Interstellar Academy. They could use a man like you.'

Jim looked at her, stunned. Before this adventure, he never would have dreamed of going to the Interstellar Academy. A grin spread across his face. Now there was nothing he would love to do more than just that!

From the edge of the deck, Silver watched, beaming as proudly as any parent.

'Just wait until your mother hears about this,' Doppler said excitedly. 'Of course, we may downplay the life-threatening parts,' he added.

'Jimmy, that was unforgettable!' B.E.N. exclaimed. 'I know you don't like touching, but get ready for a hug, big guy, 'cause I gotta hug you!' The robot reached out to hug Jim. 'Hey! You hugged me back!' B.E.N.'s metallic blue eyes glistened. 'Oh, I promised myself I wouldn't cry!' he said tearfully.

Jim smiled and turned back to Silver . . . but the old pirate was gone!

In the hangar bay, Silver was hurriedly untying the last longboat. Morph floated nearby. 'Morphy, we gotta make tracks!' Silver told his friend. He wanted to get out of there before anyone noticed he was missing.

'You never quit, do you?' a voice suddenly said. Silver flinched and turned round. Jim was standing at the entrance to the bay.

'Ah, Jimbo!' Silver laughed nervously. 'I was . . . merely checkin' to make sure our last longboat was safe and secure . . .'

Jim strolled over to the boat and tightened the knot that Silver had been trying to undo. 'Well, that should hold it,' he said.

Silver shook his head. 'I taught ya too well,' he said. He looked at Jim for a long moment. 'Now if ya don't mind, we'd just as soon avoid prison. Little Morphy here, he's a free spirit. Bein' in a cage, it'd break his heart.'

Jim hesitated. Then he punched the hatch release, opening the bay doors. Silver sighed with relief. He looked warmly at Jim.

'What say ya ship out with us, lad?' he said.

'Ship out with us,' Morph agreed, imitating

Silver's voice. He transformed into a pirate hat and placed himself on Jim's head.

'You and me, Hawkins and Silver! Full of ourselves, and no ties ta anyone!' Silver grinned.

Jim looked at him thoughtfully, then gave a wistful smile and gently removed the Morph hat from his head. 'You know, when I got on this boat, I would've taken you up on that offer in a second,' he told Silver. 'But I met this old cyborg and he taught me that I could chart my *own* course. And that's what I'm gonna do.' Jim stared out of the bay doors at the sea of twinkling stars below.

Silver came and stood at his side. 'And what do ya see off that bow o' yours?' he asked.

'A future,' said Jim. He looked at Silver with such pride and confidence that the old cyborg's eyes filled with tears.

'Look at ya! Glowin' like a solar fire,' he said. 'You're somethin' special, Jim. You're gonna rattle the stars.' Suddenly, he swept Jim into a big bear hug.

Jim's own eyes grew teary as he hugged Silver back. The two looked at each other. 'Got a bit a grease in this cyborg eye o' mine,' Silver said with a sniffle.

Morph nuzzled against Jim one last time and

burst into tears. Jim smiled and gently rubbed his belly.

'Ah, Morph . . . I'll see ya round, OK?' Jim said.

'See ya round,' Morph echoed, and flew back to Silver.

Silver looked at Morph and back at Jim. Then he quickly made a decision. 'Morphy,' he said quietly, 'I got a little job for ya. I need ya ta keep an eye on this here pup.' Silver nodded towards Jim. 'Will ya do me that little favour?'

Morph nodded happily. He nuzzled against Silver's cheek, then flew to Jim's side. Jim looked at Silver, stunned. Jim knew that Morph was more than a pet – he was Silver's best friend.

The pirate grinned and turned to leave. Then he looked back over his shoulder. 'Oh,' he said, 'and one more thing.' Silver pulled a handful of jewels from his pocket – the few he'd stashed before the treasure chamber had collapsed – and tossed them to Jim. 'For your dear mother,' Silver told him. 'To rebuild that inn of hers.' He winked at Jim and climbed into the longboat.

Jim watched as the boat was lowered through the bay doors. 'Stay outta trouble, you old scallywag,' he said.

Silver chuckled. 'Why, Jimbo, lad, when have I

ever done otherwise?' The pirate's laugh echoed through the hangar bay as Jim watched him sail off into the etherium.

Epilogue

Jim returned home to Montressor, where he, Morph and B.E.N. helped his mother rebuild the Benbow Inn. When it was finished, Jim left home again – this time for the Interstellar Academy. He'd been accepted on the strength of Captain Amelia's recommendation. Within a few years, Jim became a captain in his own right, in command of a fine crew.

But there were still some nights when he would gaze out into the etherium and see the wink of Silver's cyborg eye and hear his hearty laugh. Jim would smile softly at the memory of the old pirate who helped him find treasure – the treasure inside himself.